38250SLV00001B/11/P

LVOW13s2108200414

Printed in the USA

CPSIA information can be obtained at www.ICGtesting.com

D1417413

The Reborn

JournalStone's DoubleDown Series, Book IV

By

Brett J. Talley

JournalStone
San Francisco

JOURNALSTONE
YOUR LINK TO ARTISTIC TALENT

JournalStone books may be ordered through booksellers or by contacting:

JournalStone
www.journalstone.com

The views expressed in this work are solely those of the authors and do not necessarily reflect the views of the publisher, and the publisher hereby disclaims any responsibility for them.

ISBN: 978-1-940161-54-9   (sc)
ISBN: 978-1-940161-55-6   (ebook)
ISBN: 978-1-940161-56-3   (hc – limited edition)

JournalStone rev. date: April 11, 2014

Library of Congress Control Number: 2013958204

Printed in the United States of America

Cover Design: Denise Daniel
Cover Art: M. Wayne Miller

Edited by: Aaron J. French

For Annie, Brent, Caitlin, Elizabeth, Erin, Jeff, Joe, Kate, Krista, Kurt, Megan, Mike, Nick, Pam, Rob & Steve—thanks for trusting me enough to let me kill you.

The Reborn

It is the late summer of 2050, seventeen years after the end of the Great War, and twenty-five years after A-Day.

Chapter 1

Amanda Baker couldn't run anymore. A few months earlier? Maybe. But not now. Perhaps there's no such thing as being a little pregnant, but Amanda was heavy with child, as Sister Doris might have said.

And because she couldn't run, she hid. Locked herself in an interior room of an abandoned building somewhere north of the Heights that smelled of dried urine and dead rats, and there she waited.

Her grandmother had told her that when a storm is coming, you take shelter. You go inside, you lock yourself away, you stay down and you hide. Then you hope the monster doesn't find you. Now the monster was coming for Amanda Baker, and she didn't think hiding would do much good. Not anymore.

For nine months she had hid, since she'd let her boyfriend take her to that hospital. She should have been smarter. Never take a chance unless you know how it's going to turn out. That's what she had always said. That was what she had lived by. She could have gone to one of the clinics in Southeast. She knew where they were. She knew girls who had been to them. They'd take care of everything. They'd run the tests, tell you right where you stood, and if your baby was Clear, that's when you went to the hospital. And if it wasn't? If it was Marked or, God forbid, Reborn? Then you made a choice.

Amanda didn't have that chance now; nor did she have a choice. She had gone to the General Hospital, just like Paul had wanted. When the tests came back, she saw it in the nurse's eyes. She knew. That's when she'd started running. But she hadn't gone far; DC was the only city she knew.

Yet she ran anyway, away from her boyfriend who would have made her do it, would have made her "do the right thing," just like he always did. She'd stayed with a family that clung to the old ways, a Catholic couple who had been friends with her parents. They'd put her up, and there she'd tried to figure out what to do and where to go.

For nearly nine months, it had worked out. She had done it. She had kept her head low. But it was foolish to think she could hide forever. The General Hospital had her records. They knew who she was. One of the closed-circuit cameras was sure to make her face, or she would trigger one of the DNA sniffers all over Washington. She was bound to make a mistake.

And today, it had happened. She wasn't sure what she did, what mistake she had made. All she knew for certain was that when she heard the sirens, they were for her. If you look over your shoulder long enough, her grandmother had once said, eventually you see someone looking back.

So she ran as far as she could, as far as her swollen belly would let her go. And then she had crawled into this corner, trying to make herself as small as possible. Trying to save a life. Not her own, but her child's.

She jumped at a crash from below her, jarred out of her thoughts. The heavy tramp of booted footsteps followed. Then more explosions of noise as other doors were kicked in. She backed herself against the wall, tried to sink into it, tried to dissolve away where no one could find her. The cry of splintered wood and shattering frames flowed like rolling waves, closer and then farther away, as whoever was below searched every room, looking for her.

Then it wasn't below anymore.

She heard the crash as the door at the end of the hall was kicked in, and then the boom of every bootfall coming nearer. Another door burst at its seams, and then another, and another, each one louder than the last, pounding in her brain like a gunshot, so close she could feel it in her bones.

A shadow passed in front of the bathroom door. For a moment it lingered. She sat perfectly still, but she knew that whatever hope had been was lost, her prayers amounting to nothing but wasted breath and wasted words. Then the world caved in around her as flying pieces of wood struck her face and stuck in her hair. When she opened her eyes, two men loomed before her.

They were dressed in black—combat fatigues, heavy black boots laced high, black masks and goggles, as if they were hunting the most dangerous thing in the world instead of her. In their hands they held guns. She stared down the muzzle of one of those rifles and wondered if death was coming.

"Check her," one of them said. She couldn't even be sure which it was. One man slung his rifle over his shoulder and pulled out a DNA scanner. She tried to will her body not to betray her, but it was no use.

"It's her," the man said, slipping the scanner back in his belt. "She's Clear, but it's definitely her."

"Miss Amanda Baker," the other figure, the leader she guessed, said as he pulled out a card and started to read. "It is my duty under the Rostov Protocol of 26 U.S.C. section 5001 to inform you that you are carrying a Class 1 undesirable which we are required to terminate." He turned to his partner and nodded.

Amanda's eyes darted from one to the other. "No, no, no," she mumbled. "Please no." Her words went unheard and unheeded.

"Carry on, Sergeant."

The man who had held the scanner unholstered what could only be a gun, though of a kind she had never seen before. She tried to crawl away even as he took aim. It was no use. The man pulled the trigger.

There was no explosion, no deafening bang; only a high-pitched whistle and a flash of blue light. There wasn't even pain. But she felt it anyway, as the pulse of energy entered her abdomen. She felt it as something died inside of her, something that was part of her and yet separate all at once. Then she wished she had died, too.

The man in charge lowered his rifle. "You'll need to go to the hospital tomorrow for extraction. No charges will be filed against you for running, though if you speak about this incident, you will be arrested. I want you to know that it is very unlikely anything like this will happen again. Reoccurrence is almost unheard of. But should it, I suggest you go directly to the authorities and have it dealt with. You can't run.

"Sergeant Sadosky here will give you a card. When you go to the hospital tomorrow, present it to the Attending and he'll take care of everything. Understood?"

He didn't wait for her to respond, gesturing for his companion to finish up so they could leave. Amanda heard his words, but she was no longer listening. She saw the sergeant reholster his weapon and remove a card from his front shirt pocket. He took two steps forward and knelt down, reaching out to hand it to her. And that was the moment she had been waiting for.

She pulled the blade she had hidden from underneath her. Before the man could react, she had sliced open the back of his thigh, exactly as she had been taught. The man screamed as he fell to the ground and rolled wildly, blood pouring out of him in great spurts, painting the floor. Amanda wasn't thinking very clearly, and she couldn't focus on much, but one thing she knew was that this man, the one who had killed her baby, would be dead within minutes. To her surprise, the other man started to laugh.

"Well done, Miss Baker. Well done."

He took aim with his rifle. She didn't have time to decide whether she should be happy or sad before he pulled the trigger, adding Amanda's brains to the pool of blood that now spread slowly beneath the quivering body that lay beside her.

Chapter 2

The call had come in a little after 2 P.M. A DNA sniffer near an open-air market had scored a hit, and dispatch had assigned two teams to the case. The profile was Clear, which meant this was a runner. Two teams was surely one too many, but Dominic Miles preferred overkill. He found that a sense of inevitability made the target more docile.

They almost never fought back. They'd tell themselves later that they were paralyzed by fear, but he always thought it was simple calculation. As long as there's a chance, most people will fight. Once that chance hits zero? Then it's over. They just lay down and die.

The agents arrived in two cars, both marked like ordinary police cruisers: "*To Protect and Serve.*" Dominic set a perimeter, assigning one agent to the front of the building and one in the back. He was in no hurry. The report indicated that the girl they were looking for was eight-and-a-half-months pregnant. She couldn't run, but he figured she would try and hide. That meant she was somewhere inside this building, a five-story brick structure that had been abandoned since after the war. It was an old apartment complex, so searching it would be easy. They'd find her. It was only a matter of time.

And they had found her all right, but then the bitch had killed Sadosky. Dominic had never been particularly close with him, so it was nice, for once, to see one of them show a little spine. He'd killed her for her trouble, of course, but that was procedure. Now he had to clean this mess up and find a replacement.

He guessed the department would be doing some hiring.

* * *

Marcus knew it was bad news when he found the handwritten note on his desk. "Come see me," it said. It was signed simply, "Cap." The captain never had liked to deliver bad news over email.

The men and women in the office had learned to dread the day a handwritten note showed up on one of their desks. It was happening more and more, it seemed. There wasn't much call for policemen these days.

Marcus had felt it coming when he arrived at work. The guys had been on edge, tense, and the looks they gave him were filled with a strange mixture of sadness and relief that only now made sense. Even Haidet, normally a man who seldom shut up—particularly around Marcus, to whom he showed a special fondness—gave him only a nod before turning away. So the note was not surprising, though it was very disappointing.

Still, it could have been worse. Marcus didn't have a wife or kids at home. No mortgage to pay, nothing like that. But he had had dreams of something bigger, something better, long ago before the war. But all that seemed far away now. And if nothing else, he did have at least one mouth to feed—his own.

"No use wasting time," he murmured to himself. When he looked up, the other men and women in the precinct all suddenly became busy with other things. They had been watching him. Imagining how he must feel. They sympathized with him, but were glad it had happened to someone other than themselves.

This time, at least.

He knocked on Cap's door and didn't wait for the obligatory "come in" before he entered. The captain looked up. He didn't smile, didn't give Marcus a hearty handshake before delivering the blow. It was one thing that Marcus had always liked about Cap. He wasn't the kind of guy that would bullshit you. He wasn't the kind that would hug you close before stabbing you in the back. He gave it to you straight, and Marcus respected that.

"I'd ask you to sit," Cap said, "but I think you know why you're here."

"I'll sit anyway, if it's all the same to you."

The captain nodded a couple times and then gestured to the chair across from his desk.

"I don't know, Captain," Marcus said. "I kinda always thought we'd close this place down, turn out the lights together."

Captain Neal McKindrickson laughed and then settled into a mournful smile. "Me too. Me too. I wish that was the case, but you know how things work these days. You've been here the longest 'cept me. That means you've got the highest salary. Wasn't going to insult you by asking you to take a pay cut."

"I'm glad. I might have been tempted to accept it."

"At half what we pay you now, and who knows how long it would last. There's not a lot of future in this business."

"I think I'll take a drink, if you don't mind."

The captain reached down and removed a bottle of scotch from the lower drawer in his desk—prewar—where Marcus knew he kept it. They'd shared more than one round together in the lazy afternoons when most of the guys had already knocked off for the day. He pulled the cork clear and poured two healthy glasses, three fingers each. He dropped one in front of Marcus and held his own in the air.

"To a future with no crime."

Marcus grinned. "I'll drink to that."

"So where do you go now?"

"Well," Marcus said, swirling what was left of the brown liquid around the glass, trying to see if he could reach the rim without it spilling over. "Can't say I'd given it much thought until about thirty minutes ago."

"You had to know this was coming."

"Knowing it and accepting it are two different things. Besides, jobs—good jobs at least—are hard to come by these days." One dark drip achieved escape velocity and slid down the side of the glass. Marcus caught it with his tongue before it could get away.

"Well if you need a place to stay . . ."

Marcus cut him off with a laugh and downed his drink, slamming the empty glass on the desk. "Cap, the day I show up at your door and ask to sleep on the couch, start the suicide watch 'cause you'll know I got nothing left."

Captain McKindrickson rose and offered his hand. "Understood."

Marcus didn't hesitate to take it. The captain was, after all, a good man. A good man in a job that was becoming more difficult every day, but for reasons no one could have fathomed decades earlier.

"If you need me, I'll be at the bar."

Thirty minutes later he had made good on that promise. He was one of only two customers in the Alehouse Rock at 10:30 in the morning. The bartender didn't ask Marcus any questions. He just filled his glass and let him go. An hour and four drinks later, it was only Marcus remaining, the other patron having departed for greener pastures. Marcus didn't notice when the fellow left and didn't care, nor did he notice when the door opened and another fellow walked in. It was only when he sat down next to Marcus—and ordered water—that he took notice. The man looked at him and smiled, holding up the glass.

"On duty," he said.

"Then maybe you shouldn't be in a bar."

The man chuckled. "Depends on the job, I suppose."

"And what job brings you here?"

"Looking for a man actually, one that I was told would be here."

"Is that so? How's that working out for you?"

"Depends. You are Marcus Ryder, correct? The same Marcus Ryder who served with the 15th in Siberia during the war?"

Marcus finished his beer and called for another. For the first time he really looked at the person next to him. He was stout, but not big. Heavy, but not fat. Cut muscle, and lean too. Marcus didn't know if he was military, cop, or some combination of both. But whatever he did, he was Special Forces. Of that much, Marcus felt certain.

He had known dozens of guys who looked like him, served with hundreds of them in the war. But there was something else about this man, something that marked him as one not to be trifled with. It was the eyes. There was a coldness in them, like the wind blowing across the tundra. This man cared about something, but it wasn't the sort of thing that most people cared about. He wasn't like most people. That worried Marcus. Men like this one were meant to be feared.

"I feel special, you knowing so much about me, and I so little about you," Marcus said, coolly.

After a period of time that could only be called uncomfortable, the other man said, "You were at Luoyang, weren't you? When they finally broke through to the Golden Hall of the Khan, you were the man who killed him, weren't you?"

Now it was Marcus's turn to feel cold, to feel the ice breaking underneath him. "That's classified."

The man burst out laughing, cackling so hard the bartender on the other side of the room jumped, his obsession with the replay on the television of a particular football game interrupted.

"I like you already." He held out a hand, and Marcus took it. "I'm Dominic, Dominic Miles. I've been looking for you."

"How did you find me?" Marcus asked, choosing that over the perhaps more appropriate, "*Why?*"

"Your captain said you would be here. Or your old captain at least. I hear you've had a rough day."

"You might say that."

"Well I'm here to make you a proposition. Police work is a noble profession. Or it was, back before the war. It's not surprising that you would choose it, after your training, all you've been through, all you've learned. I was there too, man. They train you to kill. They teach you to like it. They give you every skill you need to sow death. And then when the war ends they send you back into the world with a pat on the back and a 'good luck, soldier.' They expect you just to go back to the way things were. And when they ask you on an employment application what you're good at, what your particular talents are, 'killing men' and 'making things go boom' are not usually high on the list of preferred credentials. Am I right?"

Marcus simply nodded. He was right. He guessed being a cop was a "noble profession" as Dominic put it, but it was also the only job he could get. He didn't know how to do anything else.

"But here's the thing, Marcus, it's not like the old days. We don't investigate crime anymore. We stop it before it happens. The war didn't end, my friend. The battlefield simply changed. Guys like you, guys like McKindrickson, a dying breed. But I'm here to tell ya, it doesn't have to be that way, not for you. I know what you did during the war. I know it was you that took out Khan, ended it all, stopped the fighting in its tracks. You ever think how many lives you saved with that one bullet? And then they told you that you couldn't talk about it, right? They gave you a medal you couldn't keep for a story you couldn't tell. They didn't want it to be about one man. They wanted it to be about all of us, in it together. After so many dead, I guess we needed that. We all killed Khan. We all pulled the trigger. We all fired the shot. But people remember what you did, the people that matter. And right now, they are finally ready to give you the reward you deserve."

"And what reward is that?"

"A new beginning." Dominic pulled a shield from his pocket, a badge. There was an eagle in the background, wings spread, talons out ready to strike. And crossed in front of it, two objects. One a staff, a shepherd's crook. The other a sword, long and sharp. "I am employed by an organization that you have probably never heard of, a small enforcement division under the Department of Homeland Security. We don't have a designation, at least not officially. Most people just call us the Shepherds."

"The Shepherds? Why do they call you that?"

"Because, Mr. Ryder, someone has to keep the wolves at bay."

Chapter 3

"You know, when we were kids," Dominic said as he and Marcus climbed into his SUV, "I thought we'd have flying cars by now. I thought we'd have all kinds of things."

"Maybe we would have," Marcus said, "if it hadn't been for the war. It seemed like everything just stopped then."

"You're right. The war changed everything."

Marcus nodded his head in agreement even though Dominic was wrong, and Marcus knew it. Everything had changed before the war came.

It had started with a man named Franklin Dodd Evans. Evans was a murderer, at least according to the state of Alabama. To others, he was a symbol, an example of an innocent man condemned to die.

The evidence against Evans was less than spectacular. He had known the victim, one Dale Kimbrough, and the two had had a falling out shortly before Kimbrough found himself on the wrong end of a 9 mm.

The gun was never located, but Evans was known to have purchased such a weapon at some point in his past, and his own piece was missing. Evans claimed it had been stolen some months before the murder. No one had seen Evans and Kimbrough together that night, and while Evans had no alibi beyond being alone in his trailer, there wasn't any evidence to show that he had left his home, either. It was a meager case for the prosecution, and Evans would have probably been acquitted were it not for a single strand of hair found at the crime scene.

But even that was suspect. The hair's DNA had already begun to degrade by the time the police found it. Kimbrough was killed in July. What the intense heat of an Alabama sun began, the rain from an equally intense Alabama thunderstorm had helped to complete. All that was left was one strand of Ohno STR—junk DNA that was thought to serve no real purpose and that no one outside of a handful of scientists had even heard of at the time. Yet that was all that was needed. According to the experts who testified at Evans's trial, Ohno STR was perfectly unique—it was as tied to an individual as his fingerprint, if not more so. In these experts' professional opinions, Evans was unquestionably the killer.

The jury agreed. Evans was convicted and sentenced to die. Yet he never stopped proclaiming that they'd got the wrong guy, and in the years that followed groups like The Innocence Project and Amnesty International rallied to Evans's defense, claiming that the DNA evidence was flawed. The courts were not sympathetic, and on May 15, 2002, Evans became the last man to sit in the Yellow Mama, Alabama's colorfully named electric chair. The initial jolt of electricity—which lasted in excess of thirty seconds—didn't kill him. The second only served to set him on fire. The third, however, did the trick. Evans was dead, and Kimbrough's death, vindicated.

That's how everybody remembered it, at least until the summer of 2020, the summer of the San Francisco Sandman. He was a killer of the most gruesome kind. Hunted with a knife, carving up his victims—always women—in increasingly sadistic ways. But it was one peculiar thing he did that earned him his nom d'morte; he liked to sew the eyelids of his victims shut with a needle and thread so that they might appear, were it not for the missing organs or split-open stomachs, only to be sleeping. Thus a legendary serial killer was born.

They caught the Sandman more than a year after his killing spree began. He was a bit of a prodigy as serial killers go, a seventeen-year-old drifter named Owen Danielson. Danielson denied guilt, claiming that he was an innocent man whom the desperate authorities were intent on framing. But his DNA was found on thread that had sealed the eyes of the Sandman's last victim, and it was an open-and-shut prosecution for the district attorney's office. The case likely would have lived on only in the imagination of Hollywood movie producers and horror writers were it not for an overeager intern with Amnesty International who ran a check on the Ohno STR from the Danielson case and made a startling discovery—it was a perfect match for the DNA recovered in the Evans trial. When independent scientists reviewed the intern's findings, they were shocked to find she was correct.

The result was something akin to judicial chaos. There was no question that Owen Danielson had nothing to do with the Kimbrough murder; he wasn't even born when Evans went to the chair. The conclusion seemed to be that DNA testing, at least using Ohno STR, was fundamentally flawed. And that was a problem.

Across the country, hundreds of convictions rested almost entirely on Ohno STR evidence. The use of DNA in criminal prosecutions, whether derived from Ohno STR or not, was suspended until more research could be conducted. And in a move that surprised no one, the Supreme Court unanimously declared that all convictions involving Ohno STR were to be vacated, with the accused to be retried or released. Almost universally, cash-strapped districts elected not to bother with new trials and hundreds of men and women—convicted of everything from robbery to rape to first-degree murder—were released from prison. The Innocence Project declared it the greatest day for the criminal justice system since the passage of the Eighth Amendment.

And that's when the crime wave started.

* * *

Dominic pulled off of 9th Street and onto New York Avenue heading northeast. The area had enjoyed a brief renaissance during the war, but since then it had been largely abandoned, just row upon row of empty warehouses. Dominic passed beyond them to a nearly deserted area, down a broken drive past ancient "No Trespassing" signs and a series of squat brick domes, to a warehouse behind which he parked the car.

"The old United Brick Corporation," Dominic said. "There was a time when you would never go to a place like this. Drugs, gangs, crime. Back then, there was enough business that a cop wouldn't have had to worry about losing his job. Now it's just empty. Going to waste."

Dominic hopped out. "Come on," he said before slamming the door. "This is it. I know it doesn't look like much."

The two men walked up to a side door that was innocuous other than the card scanner beside it. "We like to keep a low profile." Dominic slid a card through the reader and there was a soft click. "Nobody much comes up here anymore, and no one really even knows about the organization, so the security is pretty much for show, even if it is thorough."

A buzzer sounded somewhere inside, and Dominic pulled the door open. The warehouse didn't look all that different on the inside. The two men strode across the open, abandoned factory floor to an old freight elevator. Dominic slid his card down another reader—"Nothing more annoying than leaving this thing at home"—and they waited as the elevator car rose from the depths.

When the doors opened, it took Marcus's breath away. The interior was spotless—sheer metal walls reflected every particle of light. The two men stepped inside, and the doors closed behind them. There were no buttons to push. The car began moving down on its own for what seemed to Marcus like a suspiciously long time.

The doors opened to a small room. A man in a uniform was seated at a desk. He looked up at Dominic and nodded. Dominic jerked a finger at Marcus.

"He's with me."

The guard nodded again, and Marcus noted for future digestion that the guard's right hand remained underneath his desk, no doubt grasping the handle of a firearm of some sort. A double door opened, and Marcus followed Dominic into an open floor space that was not unlike that of the precinct. Men and women sat at cubicles, typing away at computers. There was an air of efficiency about the place, exactly as one would expect from a policing outfit. The only difference was the huge digital map of North America covering the far wall. Red lights blinked off and on across the continent, with a concentration around the DC area. The depiction of the West Coast made him shudder. It was completely blank, as dead and devoid of life as the actual piece of earth it represented.

He remembered in the old days, when he was young, that people had worried "the Big One" would come, and that California and the rest of the West Coast would simply slide into the sea. In the end, it wasn't nature that turned heaven to hell.

It was man.

* * *

The United States had long enjoyed steadily declining crime rates, which is one reason the winter of 2022 was so harsh for everyone. The Supreme Court had opened the doors of America's prisons, ostensibly to see innocent men and women go free. By the time the wave of robberies, rapes, and murders had subsided, many of those who had received a reprieve found themselves back in jail. Baffled experts in criminology and forensic psychology wondered what had happened. Were these men turned into violent criminals by their time in prison? Or had the DNA evidence—flawed though it might have been—somehow led to the right person being convicted of the right crime?

It was the Kensington Paper that changed everything, the Kensington Paper that ushered in a new era for mankind, the Kensington Paper that shook to their very foundations religion, politics, government, and philosophy. For it was the Kensington Paper that first hypothesized the existence of the Reborn.

It wasn't a paper at all, in fact. It was Erin Kensington's doctoral thesis. And she had been thorough. She had gone back into thirty years of records and collected Ohno STR results from every capital murder case that resulted in a conviction in every jurisdiction. What she found confirmed a hypothesis she had held in secret but did not dare to utter aloud.

The DNA sequence in Ohno STR recurred in many of the cases, and it always reappeared after the convicted was executed or died in prison; none of the subjects shared Ohno STR with another killer alive at the time. In an even more disturbing development, killers who shared the same DNA sequence also tended to share the same MO.

Kensington ended her dissertation in as provocative a way as possible, writing, "For millennia, mankind has searched for confirmation that there is something beyond this life, for proof that we will live again. Many believers look for a god in the sky. But God is not there. He is in our DNA, and so is our soul. And we can—and will—live again."

Of course, Kensington's findings were immediately and resoundingly rejected by the scientific community. But her thesis sparked a wave of research. Kensington followed up her study of convicted murderers with rapists, and once again, the same pattern emerged.

Soon, independent analysis began to confirm Kensington's theory. The August 2023 issue of *Time* magazine featured the Buddhist wheel of rebirth with the headline, "Reincarnation: Scientific Fact."

Reaction was as swift as it was diverse. Parts of the Middle East erupted in violent protests, with conservative Islamic clerics declaring that any notion of reincarnation was *Bid'ah*—an evil innovation. They further declared that anyone who professed a belief in reincarnation to be a *kafir* worthy of death.

The Catholic Church was less extreme, expressing both skepticism and its intent to study the matter further, while noting that there was not necessarily an inconsistency between reincarnation and Christian tradition. At the same time, Buddhism experienced an explosion of growth in the United States that it hadn't seen since its celebrity-spawned renaissance of the 1980s. Meanwhile, governments around the world began to study what this development meant for criminal courts and preserving law and order.

The implications of Kensington's research went well beyond the world of criminal justice and religious belief. Tin-pot despots and authoritarian dictators around the globe had always claimed some loose birthright that gave them an air of legitimacy. Now they began to support those assertions with "scientific" evidence. North Korea was a leading innovator in this area, with Kim Jung Un declaring himself to bear the same genetic marker as Sejong the Great, having supposedly recovered a strand of DNA from a relic of the great king housed in a museum in Pyongyang. Before long, a new wave of grave robbing and black market archeology had developed, with the world's rich and powerful paying enormous sums for proof that the blood of great men and women flowed through their veins.

And in Luoyang, a large industrial backwater in the middle of China, a man born with a blood clot in his right hand had begun to gather a legion of followers—the poor, the workers, the disaffected underclass of communist Chinese society.

They called him father, but his name was Khan.

* * *

"I've read your file, and I like what I see."

Dominic had led Marcus Ryder into an interior office—one that by its location and decoration was obviously reserved for whoever was in charge of this operation—where he was met by a black man with a face that bespoke command. They say you can read some peoples' faces like a map, that the canyons and valleys that cut across their brow and down the corner of their eyes and along the edge of their mouth can tell the story of their lives. Ryder had read this particular story before. This man had served in the war, and he had seen hard things.

"I'm glad to hear that," said Marcus.

"We don't make many hires," he said, "and when you sign on here, we expect a lifetime commitment."

It wasn't that Marcus was unwilling to take such a plunge—this job would be a blessing, one he couldn't turn down, no matter what the requirements—but the man's words still surprised him.

He didn't do a good job of hiding it either, and the man across from him, whose name he'd given as Commander John Porter, held up his hand.

"That may sound extreme, I know. But what we do here, we do in secret. And once you know that secret, you keep it forever, and we keep you. So I will certainly understand if you want to back out now. Do you need a day or two? We want to make this as easy as possible for you."

Marcus supposed he should take some time, that he should at least pretend to think it over. But he had already decided he would do whatever they wanted, so he simply nodded.

"Are you sure, son? You don't even know what you are getting into."

"And I assume you aren't going to tell me unless I agree to it? This is a sight unseen deal, right?"

Porter stared back at him.

"Then I'm in. The best friend you ever find is in a foxhole, and nothing builds loyalty like desperation. There's not a whole lot left for me to do out there, so I guess I'm in if you'll have me."

Porter dropped Marcus's file on the table and looked up at Dominic. He nodded.

"Then you're in," Porter said, never looking away from the other man. "Dominic will train you. Come on." He stood. "It's time you learned what we do here."

Chapter 4

Marcus followed Porter and Dominic back out into the open room where the other officers were gathered.

"This is the bullpen," Porter said. "Probably looks familiar to you. And it should. We do the same thing that you did in the force. Investigate leads, coordinate our operations, that sort of thing."

Porter gestured toward the large screen on the far wall. "This is what we call the Big Board. Every case we are working is marked here by a red light, the information coming from our computer mainframes in the basement. When we get a call on the tip line or when a DNA sniffer picks up a genetic trace we've been looking for, it pops up here. The blinking lights are active cases where we have leads. Solid red means we've heard nothing new in at least a week. The green lights are cleared cases; they stay up for a day. Sort of a reminder of a job well done. And if you want to, you can bring up the details of any case on the Big Board."

Porter picked up a computer pad and tapped one of the red lights. The image on the Big Board dissolved and then reformed into the picture of a young woman who couldn't have been more than twenty-five. Twenty-two, in fact, as evidenced by the birth date that was displayed beneath her photo. Bullets of information scrolled up the right column, including her last known location, suspected destination, previous addresses—the standard stuff a cop would need to know in order to find a suspect. But there was one thing missing, the thing that should have explained why a girl like this had her picture displayed on the wall of an elite law enforcement agency in the first place.

"What did she do?"

"Same thing as all of them. She ran." The image dissolved back to the graphic of the United States. Porter looked at Marcus and his face was implacable. "Have you heard of the Warren-Rostov Act?"

Of course he had. It was the law that had cost him his job, and he told Porter so.

Dominic smiled. "And it's the law that got you a new one." He waited for the truth to dawn on Marcus, until it spread across his face like ripples in a pond. "After all, someone has to enforce it."

Then it all made sense. The secrecy, Dominic's cryptic words, the reason Marcus had never even heard of this agency.

"So that girl?"

"Her name is Chloe Avondale. She's a twenty-two-year-old woman from Frederick, Maryland. She went in for prenatal care three weeks ago, and routine tests indicated that the fetus was positive for the *homo sacer* gene—a Reborn. She was scheduled to undergo the legally mandated termination procedure the next day. She never showed, and now she's on the run."

"From you?"

"From *us*," Dominic said. "If you're going to be a part of this, you've got to accept what we do here."

A wave of nausea swept over him. He grabbed the back of a chair to steady himself. "Yeah. Right. I guess I just didn't think that's what this place was all about."

"I'm not sure what you were hoping for," Porter said. "Counterterrorism? Some sort of SWAT team? You know as well as I do that we don't need that anymore, son. We don't need it because of what we do here. That girl up there, she may look sweet and innocent, and I'm sure she is. But her child's a murderer. It's not that he will be. He is, today. I know it's hard to wrap our heads around this sometimes, but the same blood that's in his body ran through a man named Darryl Reese five years ago. Darryl liked to use a knife and he liked to make it hurt. Good men like you caught him, pinned him in a back alley and shot him five times when he tried to attack a cop. Now he's back and we've got to finish the job."

"Right, right, I get it. It just takes a little getting used to."

Marcus didn't like the look on Commander Porter's face. It was one of disdain and cold judgment. Nor did he enjoy the feeling of a dozen pairs of eyes staring at him as everyone in the office had stopped what they were doing now. Whatever test was being given, Marcus was failing.

"I didn't mean any offense."

"We know you didn't," Dominic said, putting a hand on the commander's shoulder. "You just gotta understand, with the religious nuts out there and the factions down south, we all get a little sensitive about these things."

Porter exhaled. When he spoke, it was without emotion, in the flat, even tone of authority. "So you can handle it? If you can't you should tell us now. You haven't been here long, and we have ways of making you forget. At least in the short-term."

"I'm in," Marcus said. "I told you I was in, and I'm not backing down."

"Then I guess we can introduce you to our special friend, the Spiker."

Marcus followed Dominic and Porter down a side hallway into what could only be described as an armory. Assault rifles lined one wall, while body armor hung from pegs that ran along the far side of the room.

"Looks like you guys are ready for a war," Marcus said.

Dominic and Porter exchanged a glance, brief in time but filled with implication. "Sometimes, there are . . . complications," Dominic said. Porter didn't let him say more.

"You'll learn about those later. We came down here to show you this."

Porter typed a code into a keypad beside a large chest. A tone sounded, and the lid slid back. He reached inside and pulled out a weapon that looked like an old ray gun from a bad science fiction movie. It was longer than a handgun, with a rear compartment that extended back behind the wrist. Two long metal shards made up the body, tapering to a point where the barrel of a normal gun would have ended.

Porter drew back the slide on the weapon and smiled. "The T-31 Spiker. Creates a high-energy pulse in the rear of the weapon that's amplified as it travels along the parallel tracks. Fire it at an adult and the worst you get is disorientation and possible loss of consciousness, and that's if you hit them in the head. But for a fetus, it's instant death. The brain just turns off. This tool exists for one reason— humane termination. It will be your main weapon."

The commander held the gun out to Marcus and motioned for him to take it. It was lighter than Marcus expected, and it had an elegance and symmetry to it that belied its purpose.

"The rest of it is more conventional. We try and not use it."

Porter placed the weapon back in its cradle within the case and the top slid closed.

"So that's it, Ryder. That's what we do. I know you've said you are in, but I want you to sleep on it. If you still decide yes, then welcome to the team. If not, come back tomorrow and we'll take care of the memory. But whatever you do, don't try and run from us," Porter said, with a grin that was devoid of friendship or humor. "We will find you. That's what we do."

Chapter 5

The coming of Khan changed the world, but the world didn't know it until well after he had arrived. The first references to Khan in CIA documents were made by a deep-cover agent, codenamed Jade. Jade operated in northeast China, fomenting dissent against the central authorities where possible while gathering information on organic political movements. In a communique dated February 10, 2024, Jade noted the presence of a burgeoning new cult in the city of Luoyang, Henan Province.

"They follow a man," the report said, "who claims he is the reincarnated form of Temujin—Genghis Khan. Fittingly, he goes by the moniker of Khan, having no other name as far as anyone can ascertain. It's impossible to say where he came from, what his background is, or if he has any legitimate claim of ancestry to the former emperor of the world."

The report provided a detailed account of a gathering of Khan's followers that Jade was able to infiltrate—

The meeting was held in the basement of a water banquet restaurant, and the small chamber was packed full of peasants, workers, and even some minor Communist party apparatchiks. When the appointed time came, Khan had yet to arrive. A woman standing next to me asked if I had ever attended one of these events. When I told her no, she explained that Khan was always late, often an hour or more. I wondered why, until I saw the effect it had on the crowd. Their frenzy grew with every passing moment, and by the time the lights dimmed and Khan emerged from a curtain crudely drawn across a makeshift stage—

where I had no doubt he had been waiting the whole time—emotions were at a fever pitch.

But he wasn't done. For several minutes he simply stood there, staring out over the crowd without emotion, towering above us, the raised platform on which he was perched adding to the palpable sense of authority emanating from his six-foot three-inch frame. His green eyes seemed to flash and his red hair served as witness that this man was not Luoyang born.

As he surveyed those assembled, the murmur in the crowd began to grow. It rolled over itself like the ocean in a storm, colliding and crashing, chaos given form in sound, until it was no longer the hum of human voices trampling each other, but one word, repeated each time with more fervor than the last—Khan!

I admit that even I felt the energy of the room pulsating through my body, and I joined in the chant, if only to avoid being taken as an imposter.

When it seemed the crowd had reached its breaking point, Khan finally raised his right hand. Immediately, what had been an almost unimaginable roar fell to an equally unfathomable silence.

"My children," he said, his voice rippling with its own energy, "I am your father. For years without end we have served, but we were not born to be slaves. It is not our place to crawl, but to walk upright in the light. The farmer, the worker, the factoryman, upon your back this world is built. And yet you struggle in the dirt while the fat ones of the land grow thick with avarice. Our fathers call out to us from their tombs. I hear them now in the wailing wind, in the quaking of the earth. The spirits of the mighty dead return to us.

"It is written that there was a man, in the long ago, who took a broken and enslaved people and made them an empire. Before him cities fell, armies fled, and kings bowed. And his people rose. They rose as the sun in the morning, as the moon at night. They soared like the mountains, they surged like the seas.

"Has the lesson of history been forgotten? Do we not remember the glory of our past? Do we not recall the words of the great one when he passed from this world into the next?

"'When I rise, the world shall tremble.'

"He has risen, and our enemies shake with fear!

"Prepare yourself. Come to your father! For the time is approaching my brothers, when we will drive our adversaries into the sea upon a trail of blood. And on that day, I shall stamp my foot on the ground and the world will feel it quake. War now! War forever! War upon the living! War upon the dead! War until the yawning earth shall swallow them, until the nations of the world fear my name!"

The crowd roared with such devotion that I wondered if the old building in which we gathered would continue to stand. They shouted his name, their voices lost in frenzy. And all the while he remained there, surveying these people, his people. It goes without saying, I will continue to monitor this developing situation in Luoyang . . .

Jade continued to attend meetings of Khan's followers, and her missives continued to contain glowing reports of Khan's rhetorical abilities, as well as repeated recommendations that the CIA divert resources to assisting Khan in his efforts. Soon, however, Jade's reports grew less consistent both in timing and content, becoming more in the way of rambling manifestos than concise and professional debriefings. On April 11, 2024, a CIA listening post in Tokyo decoded the last communique ever received from Jade.

It read simply: "Khan is the flail of God, and soon all will know his name."

* * *

Marcus arrived at the headquarters of the organization he still knew only as the Shepherds at 8 A.M. sharp. He had every intention of taking the job. It didn't seem like he had much of a choice. He suspected they knew it too, or he would never have been picked for this position. It had been seventeen years since the war ended. If anybody had wanted to "reward him" for what he did then, they could have, and a lot sooner. But they had waited until he was desperate, until he had nowhere else to turn. It was like fate. No use fighting it.

Dominic met him at the door. "Good to see you again." The man's face exploded in a smile as he took Marcus's hand. "You ready to get started?"

"How do you know I'm going to take the job?"

The smile never wavered. "Call it intuition. This is for you."

He handed Marcus a badge. It was the same one he had shown him in the bar. Eagle, shepherd's crook and sword crossed in front. But he noticed something he had not before, a motto, written in Latin—*In Hoc Signo Spes Mea.*

"It means, 'In this sign is my hope,'" Dominic said, as if reading his mind. "The people who first formed this organization believed it was their responsibility to make the country safe enough that it could be truly free. Chaos, anarchy, crime, fear. When you have those, people will sell their freedom for a little bit of security. We provide the security without taking the freedom."

Marcus rubbed his thumb across the raised crest. "Some might disagree."

Dominic shrugged. "I guess there's always a price. Come on, let's get you loaded up. If you are ready to hit the streets, I'd like to get you out there today."

Marcus had not expected that. He figured this would be an easy day. Fill out some paperwork and go home early. But he wasn't disappointed either. He was eager to see things through Dominic's eyes.

"Sure. Let's do it."

Dominic slapped him on the back and grinned. "Perfect."

They went inside and Dominic fished a key card out of his pocket and handed it to Marcus. "Remember, if you forget that thing, it's impossible to get inside. I didn't mention this before, but there are autoguns in the ceiling tracking us every moment we are on the factory floor. If anyone ever tried to force this door. . . . So anyway, don't forget your card at home."

They rode down the elevator and Marcus followed the other man back into the armory. Dominic took a rifle from off the wall and handed it to Marcus.

"This is the XK-7. Should feel familiar to you. You probably had an XK-5 in the war."

"Yeah. I didn't even know they made a 7."

"Just for us," Dominic said. "Versatile thing. Fires the old 5.56 standard round, as well as 7.62 mm caliber if you need a little extra stopping power."

"You guys use this stuff often? I mean, you're going after teenage girls most of the time, right?"

Dominic shrugged. "Honestly, no. Almost never." He sounded more than a little disappointed. "The truth is most of this is for the psychological effect. We go in with an overwhelming show of force and use that to subdue the target. But you gotta understand, Marcus. It's not always like that. Sometimes they fight back. We've lost guys out there, even to the ones you wouldn't think were all that dangerous. But the bigger problem is the militia groups."

Marcus laughed. "Militia groups? What are you talking about?" He had worked the streets of DC for a long time and he'd never heard of a militia operating near the city. Far from it. These days, other than a few parking tickets, the occasional petty robbery, or the more common case of some kid shoplifting, there wasn't much crime on the streets. Certainly no armed gangs. And yet, Dominic wasn't laughing. He looked deadly serious.

"Marcus, there's a war going on out there. It's a secret war. It's not in the news, and the cops don't know about it. At least, not the beat cops like you. I don't have to tell you that the country's been pretty shook up since the war."

Marcus nodded his head. That much was true. The West Coast had been devastated, with pretty much everything west of Las Vegas a nuclear wasteland. And there was the South, which seemed to exercise more independence every year. Southern governors from Virginia to Texas had formed a loose organization that had taken the form of something like a quasi-shadow government. One of their first actions had been to reject the Warren-Rostov Act, the statute that mandated the termination of the Reborn. While it remained technically the law in those states, it was never enforced. And they had paid a heavy price. While other places had experienced something of a rebound as crime rates plummeted, the southern states struggled to deal with an evergrowing criminal population, especially in the wake of the economic depression that had followed the war. Yet they persisted.

"There's a pipeline that runs through Washington," Dominic continued. "People who don't want to follow the law, they head south. Now, we've got eyes everywhere. DNA sniffers, cameras, you name it. There's no way they could make the run on their own. They've got help. Our job isn't just chasing around seventeen-year-old girls knocked up by their boyfriends with the next Ted Bundy. We need to find that pipeline and shut it off. That's where these come in. Those people shoot back, and usually they are shooting to kill. Their love for human life doesn't extend to guys like me and you. So we go prepared. Add in the modular tactical body armor," Dominic said, pulling a vest off the wall, "and nobody is better armed or better protected."

Marcus held the XK-7 in his hands. He peered down the barrel, sighting a clock on the far wall. For a moment he traveled back twenty years, to the days before the war started, when the bombs fell. When the world changed forever.

* * *

Beyond a few analysts at Langley, no one in the United States paid all that much attention to the rise of Khan in the summer of 2024. All eyes were focused on Congress and the debate that was unfolding in Washington. The Warren-Rostov Act was unlike anything anyone had seen before.

The tenets of the legislation were straightforward. Science provided a vision of the future, and we would be foolish to ignore it. Thus, all pregnant women were required to undergo prenatal DNA testing of their unborn children's Ohno STR. The findings would be compared against a national database containing all previously recorded DNA information that was to be continuously updated. Every child was then divided into one of three categories. First were the Clear, those whose genetic marker was not contained in the growing database of past criminals. The Marked were the second category. Those who carried a Marked gene had, in a past life, committed crimes that, while serious, were not generally considered worthy of death. In theory, they were to be monitored, and in the event they lived a life free of criminal activity, their DNA profile would be marked as Clear. In reality, the Marked often found themselves at a great disadvantage. No one trusted them, and certainly no one wanted to hire them. Even though there were laws in place to prevent discrimination, they were rarely enforced.

Warren-Rostov declared the Reborn—those who had been murderers, rapists, or worse—unworthy of life, making it unlawful to give birth to such a person. The authors of the legislation reached back to one of the most fundamental precepts of western law to justify such a radical position—the Roman notion of *homo sacer*, the accursed man.

These were true outlaws. Such was their danger to the community that they were outside the protection of civilized authority. They could be killed by all. They could receive protection from none. In ancient times, the phrase had become synonymous with the name of another creature that was traditionally to be killed on sight—the wolf. Thus the *homo sacer* were the wolves of men.

The law united disparate forces that had never had much in common. Women's groups objected to what they saw as a loss of freedom. The Right to Life movement objected to the murder of the innocent. But the country had grown tired of political extremes in the previous decade, and a general sense of moderate malaise had set in. With the discovery of Ohno STR, no one seemed all that innocent anymore, and the mostly Christian pro-life movement was undone by something they had always believed in anyway—original sin.

On the other side, it seemed to most that terminating a pregnancy at the earliest stages was a small price to pay for a reduction in crime. The good of the many outweighed the good of the one, and women's groups had trouble articulating why they opposed steps that would lead to safer cities and nights free of fear.

And so as Khan rallied thousands to the cause of freedom for a long oppressed people, the United States instituted a criminal statute intended to end crime once and for all. No one noticed Khan's small group growing in strength and ambition, just as no one noticed as a provision in Warren-Rostov enabling the president to "take all actions necessary" to bring about the objectives of the legislation led to the creation of a new enforcement agency, one that had no name and yet a very specific mission.

Chapter 6

Marcus and Dominic rode through the streets of DC. Dominic had the wheel, while Marcus watched the city blocks pass by, seeing them each in a new light.

"It's not an easy thing," Dominic said. "My mom, she was something else. Best woman you ever met. She was a Sullivan, Irish as the day is long. Loved the Church, man. Prayed the rosary every day. Must have spent five hours a week at confession. I wonder sometimes, what she'd think, if she knew what her son was doing. Ever feel like your whole life has been a disappointment? That's what I think sometimes. Bullshit, huh? Yeah, bullshit. Not that it matters."

"Have you ever asked her about it?"

Dominic stared out over the steering wheel, his jaw clenched. "Nah, man. It didn't work out that way."

In an instant, Marcus regretted bringing it up.

Dominic went on. "You know how some people always want to move to south Florida when they get old? For my mom, it was California."

"I'm sorry," Marcus said.

"Forget about it. You didn't know. We all lost somebody. Anyway, when the bombs hit, I joined up the next day. I knew she was gone. Just felt it, you know what I'm saying? Lots of people never gave up hope. To this day, I hear there are expeditions that head out from Las Vegas to L.A. Just looking for people who made it. Or maybe looking for the bodies of the ones who didn't. I don't know. For me, I just wanted revenge. It kept me going in the war. Every day I went out there for her. And every day I came back so I could go out again—for her. It took a lot to get over that when I got back to the States. And how about you, Ryder? Why'd you join the service?"

Marcus shrugged. "I didn't know what else to do."

Dominic started to laugh. "I guess that makes two of us."

They cruised through the deserted parts of Washington, what had been the worst of the slums before the war. The residents had moved toward downtown, a reversal of the migration that had been pushing the poor farther and farther away from the city center for decades. DC had emptied after the bombs fell on California. With American ICBMs raining down on Beijing, Shanghai, Shenzhen, and Guangzhou, there weren't many who bought the government's claims that the Eastern Seaboard was protected by a nascent SDI system that, unfortunately, had never been fully deployed.

But the bombs never came, and a nuclear war eventually morphed into a more traditional one. Still, there were many who had started a new life in simpler places. Washington had lost its allure for them. The ones who did return in the hopes of taking part in a post-war economic boom—one that never really came either—found themselves living in former luxury apartments for a fifth of what they had once brought.

The effect rippled throughout the town, and DC was left with a crescent-like swath of emptiness that capped the northern part of the city. No one much came here anymore, unless they had something to hide. That's why Dominic would often cruise these streets when nothing else much was going on, and it was why he had brought Marcus with him to that place on his first day on the job.

"I think they'll tear all this down eventually. They've been talking about it for years. Money's never there. Like most things. But it's always worth coming up here. You never know what you might find."

The dashboard computer flashed on, accompanied by a ringing tone. Dominic reached down and tapped the screen. A woman's face filled it, her hair pulled back tight in a way that made her look older than she must have been.

"Sir," she said, "our recon team reported back on that clinic you spotted last week. They got a hit on a Krista Duarte, a runner who disappeared a little over three months ago. It's enough to go in and search the place. A warrant was issued this morning. Transferring to your handheld."

"Roger. We'll go take a look and report back. We should be able to handle it, but call in Harrington's team for backup."

"Will do, sir."

The screen went blank and Dominic turned to Marcus and grinned. "Finally. Some action."

He spun the SUV into a fishhook and gunned the engine, the sound echoing through the empty streets, bouncing off the walls of abandoned buildings.

* * *

Analysts in Washington were unimpressed with the rise of Khan, whom one higher up in the CIA had dubbed the Luoyang Lunatic. But Khan's influence spread beyond Asia, and he even began to achieve some adherents in the West, particularly in an America that was in the midst of a spiritual crisis. But no one knew how great Khan's power was in the domed hills and open plains of Western China, not until the Great Eastern March began.

Vague reports initially called it an antigovernment protest, though the reason behind it was unknown and, for most people, unimportant. Just one more angry mob the oligarchs in Beijing would have to put down. And with the precise regularity of Chinese communism, soldiers were deployed west to disperse the protestors and liquidate the leaders of the movement. It was only when the rank and file of the People's Liberation Army killed their commanders and threw their support behind Khan that the world sat up and took notice.

The march began in Lanzhou, the city where Khan had gone to rally his western adherents to his cause. They flowed by the thousands like the waters of the Yellow River, following the valley to Baotou in Inner Mongolia.

Then they turned toward Beijing.

On October 1, 2024, Khan's forces passed through the Badaling Gate of the Great Wall, forty miles from the capital. The city was indefensible, particularly with the PLA in complete disarray. The Central Committee ordered a general withdrawal from the city, until such time as it could determine the loyalty of its soldiers. Khan entered Beijing on October 5 to no resistance.

The world economy was thrown into turmoil. The Dow Jones lost twenty percent of its value in a single day of trading. Analysts, politicians, journalists—no one had predicted it, and no one had seen anything like it. Some began to speak of a new order, a dangerous unknown. But then the PLA launched its counterstrike.

They stormed into Beijing, prepared to meet a dug-in enemy they would have to remove in house-to-house combat; bombing the City of Mao was not an option. But things did not go as the military leaders and Politburo had expected. They did not find an army ready to fight, ready to resist to the death.

They found something much worse.

The soldiers who entered Beijing that day reported that the streets were empty, the normal roar of the beating heart of the city, silent. They marched down the boulevards with nothing but the desolate sound of a north wind and their own footfalls for comfort. Khan and his men were gone. They had melted away, disappeared into the west once again. Had they not left behind a pyramid of 500,000 human heads in the center of Tiananmen Square, you might never have known they had been there.

Chapter 7

The two men arrived at a nondescript office building at the outskirts of the inhabited part of the city. The place serviced the poor, or at least that was how the Oblinger Clinic billed itself. Dominic suspected something more nefarious was going on, and he told Marcus as much.

"Last week," he said, "we tracked a runner named Amanda Baker from this location into the deserted part of town just north of here. We are pretty sure she was getting medical care from these guys, illegally of course. I tell you what, it's always these clinics. Fly-by-night shops. Religious quacks. The main hospitals would never do this shit."

Marcus nodded absent-mindedly. "So what's the plan?"

Dominic glanced at his watch. "Harrington's crew should be here soon. We wait for them to arrive, and then we walk in the front door and serve our warrant."

"You expecting trouble?"

Dominic grinned. "Absolutely. They know exactly what they are doing in there. They'll fight. They'll stall. Probably try and sneak some girls out the back. Whatever it takes."

Dominic glanced at Marcus and saw the doubt etched across his face.

"You sure you're ready for this?" he asked, just as Harrington rolled up beside them with their support team and a warrant.

"Yeah," Marcus answered. "As ready as ever."

"Good. Let's go."

They got out of their vehicle and Dominic walked over to the driver's side of the car where Marcus assumed Harrington was seated. The person inside lowered the window and Marcus was surprised to see it was a woman. The two talked in hushed, inaudible tones. Then Dominic nodded once and tapped his hand twice against the door before looking up and smiling. "We are good to go."

Marcus followed behind Dominic as they walked down the concrete path which cut through a dying field of brown grass and dry mud holes. Dominic reached into his pocket and removed a thin black cylinder that resembled a fountain pen. He clicked a button on the side and a spike sprang from the end. He jammed it into the ground next to the path, a dim red light blinking slowly at its top.

"DNA sniffer," Dominic said, answering the unasked question. "When we go in, they are going to come out. This little baby will make them, and then Harrington and her crew can process them."

They approached the front door of the clinic. Dominic reached down and clicked off the safety on the assault rifle slung around his neck.

"You'll want to be ready."

Marcus followed suit, and Dominic opened the door.

The room was half-full with waiting patients. An old vid screen hung from the wall, silently broadcasting a national news channel, the lack of sound or subtitles rendering it useless. Marcus made a mental note that doctors' offices were the only place in the world you could still find paper copies of magazines. None of the patients were reading them though. All eyes were on the two heavily armed men standing in the doorway.

Dominic paid the civilians no mind, striding across the room toward the nurses' station against the back wall. Marcus had more trouble, and he found himself glancing from one terrified woman's face to another. Some held tightly to the men with them, presumably the fathers of the unborn children they carried. Others held only to themselves; they had no one.

Marcus was only a quarter of the way across the room before Dominic's prediction came true and one of the women stood up quietly and slipped out the front door. It seemed that with every step Marcus took, another one followed. Some tried to leave discretely, tiptoeing silently across the tiles. Others made no effort to conceal their escape. It didn't matter. Marcus wouldn't stop them, and Dominic was paying no attention. He was standing in front of the middle-aged woman who was apparently the intake nurse, his arms spread more than shoulder-width apart as he leaned on the desk, his rifle banging against the edge.

Marcus sidled up to Dominic and felt his hand slip down to the grip on his gun. Dominic spoke first.

"Hello, ma'am," he said politely. "We're police officers."

"I can see that," she said. Marcus noticed the crucifix hanging from her neck. "Is there something I can help you with? This is a health clinic, as I'm sure you noticed. We've done nothing wrong."

"Then you should have nothing to hide. Mind if we take a look around?"

"Unless you have a warrant, I am afraid I'm going to have to ask you to leave. Your weapons are making our patients uncomfortable."

Dominic turned and glanced at the empty waiting room.

"That's funny," he said, "you don't seem to have any patients."

"And that would be the point, wouldn't it?"

Dominic looked down at the desk and chuckled, wiping his hand across the polished glass. He reached inside his pocket and pulled out a piece of paper, dropping it in front of the woman.

"There you go."

The nurse picked up the document from its corner like it was radioactive. "I'll have to have the doctor take a look at this before I can let you come back here."

"Look lady," Dominic said, finally losing his patience, "you can either . . ."

He didn't finish his sentence. He glanced up, something clicked, and he grabbed Marcus and threw him to the ground just as the wall behind the other man exploded in a shower of broken wood and plaster.

Time slowed. The smell of gunpowder filled Marcus's nostrils, and his heartbeat tripled. For a moment he was back in the Longmen Valley, pinned down by heavy machine-gun fire from positions he could neither see nor do anything about. Beside him, Dominic lifted his gun above his head and fired wildly in the direction of the shooter, sweeping back and forth in a desperate attempt to silence him. But as soon as he stopped, the world exploded again, and Marcus pulled himself into a ball, jamming his hands against his ears, praying for it to stop. Only when Dominic smacked him hard across the face did he return to the present.

"Don't bug out on me! I need you here, *now.*"

Marcus stared dumbly at Dominic as he returned fire, his efforts serving only to hold the gunman at bay. As the unknown assailant fired again, Dominic turned to Marcus.

"Here's the plan!" he shouted above the roar of a machine gun. "I'm going to fire back. When I pin him, you take a position above the desk. He'll pop back out to shoot, and that's when you plug him! You get me?"

Marcus nodded weakly, and he could feel as much as see the doubt in Dominic's eyes. Dominic nodded once before lifting his gun above the desk and firing blindly.

Whether it was his training kicking in or some survival instinct he'd occasionally thought he'd lost, Marcus picked himself up and took a position with his gun propped against the edge of the counter. He could feel the heat from the shells flying from Dominic's rifle, though he didn't actually register the sound of the individual shots. It had all become one tempestuous roar, like the ocean in a storm.

Dominic stopped firing. Marcus spotted movement to his left, a flash of white just out of the corner of his eye. He spun and fired in one movement, three precision shots. And then nothing. A full minute went by before he registered the sound of a voice screaming out of Dominic's radio. It was Harrington, ordering her men to charge the front door.

"Stand down," Dominic said finally. "Secure in here. Just cover the exits and make sure nobody gets out."

Marcus kept his eyes trained downrange, tracking back and forth with his gun, looking for movement. The nurse who they'd been talking to was dead, her body lying behind the counter. He wasn't sure who shot her or how it happened. He supposed explanations didn't really matter. He barely flinched when Dominic clapped his hand down on his shoulder.

"Good work. Let's check out the back. And take it slow."

The two men inched toward the door of the hallway leading to the rear of the clinic, guns raised. It would have been suicide for anyone in the other room to open it, though Marcus suspected anything was possible at that point.

Dominic reached out and opened the door, jerking it wide. He moved quickly to the opposite wall, never taking his eyes off the sight of his gun. He gave the sign for clear, and Marcus stepped through.

The room looked like the warzone it had become. Bullet holes had ripped the wall apart—Dominic's doing, of course—and a heavy haze of plaster hung in the air. Loose papers floated on it, and Marcus thought they couldn't have done more damage with a grenade. After a few steps they found their former adversary.

She was young, probably in her late twenties, and her white uniform was now a dark shade of red, three circles of crimson growing from each of the three holes Marcus had put in her chest. She was still breathing. Or wheezing at least, bloody spittle pouring down her mouth and pooling along the crevice of her collar bone. Her eyes were wide, the light dimming with every breath. They locked on Marcus for a moment, and then she was gone.

Dominic kicked the gun away from her dead hand and spat out a curse. Then he continued down the hall. After a moment's pause, Marcus followed. They turned a corner to find a man in a white lab coat. One hand was raised as if in mockery of a hello. The other was jammed into his pocket.

"Gentlemen, please!" he cried, shaking so much that Marcus wondered how he could even stand. "This is a hospital. You've no reason…"

Dominic fired twice. *Pop-pop.* The man crumpled to the floor.

Marcus simply reacted. He spun his gun around, and now Dominic's head was in his crosshairs. Dominic saw this in his peripheral vision. His eyes narrowed, nostrils flared.

"Stand down, soldier!" he roared.

Instantly, Marcus dropped the gun to his side.

"You shot him," he mumbled. "You just shot him."

Dominic glared back, and in that instant Marcus had never felt more ashamed.

"Let me tell you something. This ain't no game of cops and robbers. This is real life. This is a war, just like the one we fought. They kill one of ours, we take out ten of theirs. That's the way we win. That Baker girl I told you about, the one who led us here? She's the reason you got a job. She killed my partner with a knife. Stuck him right in the artery in his leg. Now where do you think she learned to do that? So don't give me any of your do-gooder bullshit. Besides," he said, walking over to where the dead man lay, "he was armed."

Dominic kicked the doctor's hand out of his pocket. It still held the semi-automatic he'd been clutching.

He walked over to Marcus and put a finger in his face. "I saved your life today. Don't forget that. But you ever point a gun at me again, and I won't be so forgiving. Understood?"

He let the words hang in the air for a moment. He wasn't looking for a response and Marcus didn't give one. Then Dominic pushed the button on his comm and gave the all clear, leaving Marcus behind in the hallway, death all around him.

The two men walked back out the front door and into the late morning light. Harrington was waiting on them. She removed her tactical helmet and shook her ponytail free. Marcus couldn't help but note that she was very attractive.

"Thought I was going to have to come in there and save your ass, Dom."

"And then I took care of it like always. You process the ones that came out the front?"

Harrington nodded. "Three were Clear. We dealt with the rest. Johnson debriefed them. Said they'd heard about this place through word of mouth. Place where they didn't ask questions. And cheap too, apparently. Not sure how they kept the doors open based on what the girls told us. Anyway, none of them had even tried a real hospital. That's why the Clear girls were here. They didn't want to take the chance."

"And the ones that went out the back?"

Harrington shook her head and wiped her brow with the back of her hand. "Nobody came out the back."

"You gotta be kidding me."

"Just telling you how it went down. Rodriguez had point back there. Said when he heard the gunshots he expected to collar a bunch. But nothing."

"Could they have slipped around him?"

"Impossible. He had eyes on the only exit. If they'd come out there, he'd have seen them."

Dominic glanced at Marcus. He was confused, and Marcus could see it. He breathed deep, frowned, and turned back to Harrington. "All right. Have your guys search the place again. Strip the CPUs and torch everything else."

"Yes sir."

As Harrington turned and walked away, barking orders to her team, Dominic looked at Marcus.

"That make sense to you?"

"What? That nobody came out back?"

Dominic nodded.

"Doesn't make sense at all. That gunman was pinning us down. Trying to hold us there. Buying time. They had to be doing something back there."

"Yeah. And a full waiting room in the front and no one in the back? Doesn't add up. Well, at least you know what we are dealing with."

"So now what?" Marcus asked as the two men reached their vehicle.

"Well, we're done here. We go back on patrol and Harrington and her guys take care of this place. They'll gather up the computers, any documentation they think is interesting. And then they'll burn the place."

Marcus flinched. "Burn it down?"

Dominic shrugged, jerking open the driver's side door. "Asset forfeiture," he said. "We don't leave anything behind when we can help it. We find their resources, we destroy them. No mercy. Part of this job is sending a message."

As he climbed inside the car, Marcus wondered what else this job might entail.

Chapter 8

It all seemed like a dream. A week before Marcus had been sitting at his desk in the Fifth Precinct, with nothing more exciting than a serial shoplifter plaguing Southwest to keep him busy. And today it felt like he had dove headfirst into a very dark pool that had no bottom. Down, down, and down into a world he had never known existed. One where a war raged. Complete with dangerous enemies who—in death at least—didn't seem all that different from him, and innocent victims, if anyone in this world could ever be considered innocent.

Not that Marcus was complaining. For the first time in a long while he felt needed. He felt like he was part of something bigger than himself.

And he certainly wasn't a denier, not like so many others. He had friends and even family—such that either existed in his life—who had never accepted the truth about how things really were. They never believed in the Reborn. Couldn't even accept that it was possible. That seemed to be the thing that united them, the deniers. It wasn't evidence they wanted or proof they lacked. Argument wouldn't sway them, nor was it received with an open mind or a listening ear. They simply could not believe it. Not would not, mind you, but *could* not. It was as anathema to their worldview as rain that fell up or $2 + 2 = 5$. To face the truth, to truly conceive it, would shatter them.

Marcus thought often of a television show he had seen years ago. Before the war, even. It was on one of the twenty-four-hour news channels, one of the right-wingers. They had been debating what they were calling the "reincarnation gene." It had been a Harvard professor and a minister of one of the big California churches. The preacher's name had long disappeared from Marcus's mind, burned away in the fires of the war.

But Marcus remembered the interview being something of an event, the showdown between these two men, representatives of two opposing factions. And people had watched. People didn't know what to believe and they needed guidance. They had gotten it that night.

The Harvard professor toyed with the poor man. It seemed he had all the facts on his side. He had the studies—peer-reviewed and duly published in respected journals. He had the overwhelming weight of the scientific community behind him. And he had the technical explanation of how the reincarnation process worked, clothed in nearly unintelligible scientific jargon.

The preacher, on the other hand, had faith—and little else. He spoke of God's plan, of personal responsibility. He talked about the innocence of youth and how the son should not bear the sins of the father. He talked about the kind of world we'd live in if the professor was right, and he rejected that world, out of hand and without hesitation.

Some were swayed; Marcus was sure of that. But he wasn't one of them. He believed in the Reborn from that day forward. And since he also believed in justice and getting what you deserve, he supported the Warren-Rostov protocol when it was announced. A killer deserved to die, more than once if necessary.

He'd been 17 then. A-Day was less than a year away.

* * *

Marcus had always heard that animals can sense pending disaster. Rats leave doomed ships. Dogs hide before a storm. Wild beasts of all kinds flee from a coming earthquake. And while he was sure humans lacked that sense when it came to natural disasters, of the manmade variety he felt differently.

That summer before A-Day, people knew something was coming.

The world was obsessed with Khan. There was no story but the China story. What had happened in Beijing that October had captivated news stations, intellectuals, politicians, the common man, artists, old people, young people, and all people in-between. No one had seen anything like him, nor heard of anything like him except in dusty old history texts and Hollywood movies. Khan was more myth than man. He was a hero to some, an archvillain to others, a comic book figure to all. But a *real* one.

The cult of Khan grew, even as the man himself disappeared into the interior of China. He wasn't seen or heard from for many months. Some said he was dead. Others said he was waiting, biding his time until he could launch a new attack on the Chinese east coast.

There didn't seem to be much hope for another attack immediately after the retreat from Beijing. Li Yuanchao, the General Secretary of the Communist Party, had promised revenge on Khan and all who supported him. The American government assumed that reprisals would be swift and with a brutality even more terrible than what Khan had unleashed. The president urged restraint.

To the shock of everyone, the Chinese complied.

The PLA advanced as far as Guangzhou in the south and Harbin in the north. They went no farther. The implication was clear. China, with all its military might, had lost complete control over its interior, and it had no confidence in its ability to reassert that control.

The schadenfreude across the Pacific was palpable. The Americans had watched as the Red Dragon had grown in power and influence over the last few decades. And while the latest developments in the Orient were met by official concern, many expressed glee at China's precipitous fall. To many, Khan was a godsend. And it was this mindset that started the road to A-Day. The Chinese had been looking for a scapegoat. Now they had the perfect one—the United States government.

What started as muted propaganda was soon full-blown accusations that Khan was a CIA plant. On May 1, the Ministry of State Security—the Chinese secret police—released a report detailing clandestine operations within eastern China conducted by American spies. According to the report, these operations were meant to destabilize the Communist government and foment a civil war.

Chief among these operations was the purported cultivation of a young dissident named Chen Yat-sen, the man who would become Khan. Government sponsored rage followed the report's release, with American interests burned throughout the country, while the Beijing embassy was razed. It is a testimony to the desperation of the

Chinese that the ambassador and all consulate staff were summarily executed.

This was an act of war.

Condemnation was swift, and UN resolutions were hastily drafted demanding that the Chinese cease hostilities and bring those responsible for the attacks to justice. In return, the Politburo declared that the United States was the aggressor nation, and swore that it would have revenge for the Beijing Massacre. It gave the United States a deadline of twenty-four hours to admit her role in the rise of Khan.

That was June 17, 2025—the day before the world ended.

Chapter 9

"You did good today, even if you did threaten to shoot me."
Dominic downed his coffee and raised his cup in the direction of
the waitress. "The omelets are great here."

They'd stopped at a diner a few blocks down from the clinic
for a late breakfast/early lunch. Dominic was hungry and he'd
eaten at the place often.

"Sorry about that. Instinct, you know?"

The girl filled Dominic's cup to the rim before turning to
Marcus. "Need a top-off, hun?" she asked, even though he was
probably a good ten years older than her. Marcus couldn't help
but wonder if she was Marked. It was no guarantee, of course.
Jobs were hard to come by these days and even those lucky
enough to be Clear were happy to find employment of any kind.
Still, he wondered.

"Sure."

"And I'll have an omelet," Dominic said. He looked at
Marcus and added, "Make that two."

As the girl walked away he gestured toward Marcus with his
coffee cup. "You were rattled, is all. First time you killed anybody
since the war?"

Marcus swallowed a laugh. "First time I've shot at anybody.
First time I've been shot at. Hell, I haven't drawn my weapon but
twice, maybe three times in the last ten years."

"You get rusty," Dominic said. "I'm lucky you were as sharp
as you were. You put that shooter down, no problem."

Just like that Marcus was staring down at her again. Watching as the life fled from her eyes. In another world, in another place, he would have been happy to meet a girl like that. Now she was dead, and he had killed her.

"She'd have killed you if she got a shot," Dominic said. "Don't forget that. She was delusional. They all are."

The waitress returned and dropped the two omelets in front of them. Dominic dug right in.

"You ever think why they do it, the runners?"

Dominic leaned back in the booth, looking as thoughtful as one possibly could with a mouthful of food. He swallowed, took a drink of his coffee, and sighed.

"I've thought about it. Thought about it a lot. You know, I heard this story once, about a guy named Jackson Kittredge, I think was his name. Something close to that. This was back decades ago. Kittredge was a pretty interesting guy, and after he died his son wrote a biography of the man. You see, Kittredge was one of those people who had it all. Kids. Tall, brunette, beautiful wife. Nice business that earned him a good living. But for whatever reason, he wasn't happy." Dominic took another bite of his eggs. "You ever had one of those days where you wish you could just get in a car and drive?"

"Sure."

"Well I guess Kittredge had one of those days. He just had the guts to do something about it. One day, he woke up in the morning. Took a shower, walked out his front door and disappeared. Except he didn't get in a car and drive. He hopped a freight train and rode it till it stopped, a thousand miles away from where he started. He carried enough cash with him to rent a place for a while. Then he got a job working as a stock boy in a local grocery store. Turned out the owner was tall, brunette, and beautiful. You can probably see where this story is going."

"He married her?"

"Yep. Married her, lived happily ever after. That is, until the cops showed up at his house one day. You see, if nothing else, you couldn't say that Kittredge was a bigamist. Turns out that the cops had tracked him to his new town and had come to arrest him for the murder of his wife—the first one. See, that day he left, his wife just so happened to up and die."

"He killed her?"

"Well, that's what the cops thought. There was really no evidence that he did it, other than the fact he disappeared the day of the murder. But nobody else had a motive. The only thing that had been taken from the house was a locket that Kittredge had given his wife on their wedding day, and there was nothing particularly valuable about it. So she was dead, and he was in jail. They took him to trial, and he testified in his own defense. Said he had no reason to kill his wife. All he wanted was to start over. His life had never felt like his own, and he needed a second chance. 'You only live once,' he said. And he wanted to do it right."

"What happened?"

"The jury acquitted him. Let him go. He went back to his new wife and they went back to living their own lives together."

"Wow," Marcus said as Dominic polished off the rest of his omelet. "But what does that have to do with the runners?"

Dominic wiped his mouth and downed his second cup of coffee. "I hadn't finished," he said. "A couple years later, Kittredge's wife was cleaning out an old chest that they kept in the basement. When she got to the bottom, she found a small envelope. Do you know what was inside?"

"What?"

"The locket."

"Seriously."

"Mmmhmm."

"So he did kill her."

"Of course he did."

"What did she do then?"

"She put the locket back into the envelope, sealed it up, and threw it in the bottom of the chest. And she never said a word, not until the day she died when she told her son the story."

"But why would she do that?"

"Why'd she hide a murderer? Why did she protect somebody that was a danger not only to herself but to society? Why did she lock away the truth and continue to live with this man who she knew had something terribly wrong, something broken inside of him? There's only one answer I can think of."

"She loved him," Marcus whispered.

"That's exactly right. She loved him. And I will tell you this—there is nothing in this world more dangerous than love. People will lie for it, they'll cheat for it, and they will kill for it. And that's why we have to be so careful. Those girls out there, they are motivated by only one thing: love. They are blinded by it, and they will put you down if they have to in order to protect it.

"Now," Dominic said, "are you going to eat that omelet?"

Chapter 10

Sunday, June 18, 2025, started off like most any other day—tailor-made to be forgotten. Instead, at 7:15 A.M. Eastern, before most of Washington, DC, had even begun to wake, FLASH traffic from United States Strategic Command alerted the president that the Chinese were fueling Mao ICBMs and would have launch capability in less than an hour.

Before the president had even finished reading the message, the machinery of nuclear war—honed to a diamond point by decades of Cold War paranoia—began to turn. NORAD and Strategic Bomber Command went to DEFCON 2. Submarines off the Kamchatka peninsula were ordered to stand ready to deliver their Trident III missiles against selected targets along the Chinese coast. Meanwhile, two men held the fate of millions in their hands.

The president of the United States called the Chinese premier.

The premier responded with shock. He had not ordered his missiles to fuel or prepare for a launch. He had no knowledge of these actions. As the president listened, he believed the scared little man on the other line. But then he received a message that made all of it irrelevant.

"Mr. Premier," he said, "I have in my hand a decrypted message from Strategic Air Command. It tells me that while we have been on this call, ten Mao missiles were launched toward the west coast of the United States. I suggest you get yourself out of Beijing." Then he hung up the phone.

Orders were delivered that no commander ever expected to give to men who were wholly unprepared to carry them out. And yet carry them out, they did. A counterstrike was launched against the Chinese cities of Beijing, Guangzhou, Shanghai, Shenzhen, Shantou, and Tianjin. And as American missiles passed Chinese ones in the air, the president ordered an evacuation of the west coast of the United States.

There was no stopping the bombs. Expansions of the nation's nascent ballistic missile shield had been mothballed a decade before, put aside for domestic projects deemed of a higher priority. To the extent it functioned at all, the shield only effectively covered an area from the Eastern Seaboard to the Mississippi River, and no one knew if this limited system would even work.

That left thirty minutes for an evacuation. Thirty minutes—at most—was all the time it would take for the hypersonic weapons of man's doom to reach their targets. All flights into western cities were diverted. Airports were ordered to fuel, fill, and launch all available aircraft immediately. Military bases emptied, with transports laden with soldiers and their families heading east. Trains were filled to capacity and sent rocketing off at max speed. Even ships were used, though, in the end, they were too slow to escape the blast radius.

In the grand scheme of things, it was a miniscule number of people who were saved. The vast majority never even knew about the launch or the evacuation order. They were vaporized in their beds at 5:39 A.M., Pacific Time, when ICBMs detonated over San Diego, Los Angeles, Anaheim, San Jose, Fresno, Sacramento, San Francisco, Portland, Seattle, and Vancouver. The retaliatory American strike followed only ten minutes later.

Hundreds of millions were dead. The EMP shockwaves fried every unprotected electrical device from the coast of California to the Mississippi River, plunging half the country into a blackout that would not be fully lifted for years. The economic, technological, and human cost from that single day—called A-Day by those who lived through it—set the human race back decades.

The world waited for the next hammer to drop, waited for the Chinese to launch another salvo of missiles. But instead, silence.

That is, until a broadcast was beamed from an isolated location in the wilds of western China. It spoke of the horrors of the old communist regime, of the evil it had inflicted on the world and on China by condemning mankind to a nuclear holocaust, and it thanked the Americans for removing the threat once and for all. It then declared the beginning of a new China, a new capital in Luoyang, and a new supreme leader who, freed from interference by his enemies on the coast, promised to restore the nation to its greatest glory. He needed no title, for he already bore it.

He was already Khan.

* * *

They were finishing their coffee and Dominic was cleaning his plate when they got the call. A report had come in through the Citizen Safety Hotline, a see-something-say-something deal that offered rewards in exchange for information on suspicious behavior. It had taken them somewhere that Marcus had never expected—into the center of a DC suburb on the Virginia side, the kind of place where nice, upper-middle-class people lived. The kind of place you didn't find the Reborn. The kind of place that runners didn't run from. In his heart, Marcus hoped it was a mistake.

On the way, he had dialed through the radio stations in the car, looking for news on the events at the clinic. "I'm not sure what you are looking for, but you probably aren't going to find it," said Dominic. And he was right. The closest Marcus came was a story about the clinic burning down in what was termed an "accidental fire." According to the reporter, three bodies were found in the ashes, all having succumbed to smoke inhalation. Dominic chuckled when he saw the look on Marcus's face.

"How is that possible?"

"When's the last time you heard about a gunfight in this town? A murder? A police shootout? Can you even remember one?"

And in truth, Marcus couldn't.

Dominic turned down off of the highway onto an idyllic lane that led into McLean.

"It's all about information control. People who live in places like these," Dominic said, gesturing to the row upon row of perfect houses. "They don't want to know anyway. We feed the reporters the information they need, and they deliver it. It's a perfect relationship."

"And what about the girls? Don't they say anything?"

"No. They never talk. They want to forget. And they know that we'd find them. I guess I shouldn't say never. But who would believe them? Wild conspiracy theories. Secret government organizations." He grinned. "It's preposterous."

Dominic pulled into the driveway of a two-story Colonial with a wrap-around porch and a three-gabled front.

"So here's the deal," he said. "We've got a warrant to search the place, but we go in light. No rifles, just sidearms and spikers. A Dr. Joe Davis and his wife Kate live in that house. They've got money, and they've got connections. We are going to do this one by the book. Got it?"

Marcus didn't quite know what "by the book" meant with these guys, but nodded anyway. "I got it, but it doesn't seem right. Why would these people be mixed up in this?"

"It's less unusual than you'd think. People like the Davises run girls down south into the Carolinas, Georgia, Alabama. Places that we can't reach."

"So what do we have to go on? What did the call say?"

Dominic pulled out his gun and popped out the clip. He checked it once, saw that it was full, and slammed it back in. "Said that the Davises keep odd hours. Made them suspicious. Two weeks ago, they got home at 3 A.M. Brought a girl into the house. Neighbors were watching. They'd never seen her before, and the Davises have no daughters. And it wasn't the first time. In my book, that can mean only one thing." Dominic gestured toward the house. "The Davises are smugglers, and it's time we shut them down. Come on."

He jumped out of the car and slammed the door behind him. Marcus followed, but they were only halfway up the sidewalk when the front door opened. A woman stepped out, middle-aged but still attractive, toweling off her hands.

"Can I help you gentlemen?"

"Just want to ask you a few questions ma'am," Dominic said, flipping open his badge and then quickly stowing it away in his pocket. The woman chuckled nervously.

"Well of course. I hope there's not a problem. My husband and I were just cleaning up after lunch."

"This should only be a minute."

"Well can I ask what this is about?"

"Please ma'am, it would be better if we discussed this inside. We do have a warrant, but I'd rather not get into that kind of thing."

A pale terror slipped over her face as the color drained away. "All right then. Come in."

She turned away and led the two men through the door. Dominic looked at Marcus and winked. They followed her into a well-appointed foyer that branched off in three directions— upstairs, into a living room with a wood-burning fireplace, and toward the kitchen. The trio continued on into the latter of the three. Dr. Davis was standing in the center of the room, leaning against a middle island, a cup of coffee in one hand and the Washington Gazette—one of the old-fashioned papers that had popped up after the electronic holocaust of A-Day—in the other.

"Oh," he muttered, looking from his wife to the kitchen pantry, to Marcus, and then Dominic. "I'm sorry. I didn't realize we had . . . guests."

"It's all right, sir," Dominic said, shifting the belt on which hung his gun in a manner that the doctor couldn't miss. "I'm sure we were unexpected."

"Well," the doctor said, regaining his composure, "what can we do for you gentlemen today? I've played golf with the Chief of Police on more than one occasion, so obviously I'm happy to help."

Dominic smiled too broadly for it to be sincere. "Actually we don't work for him. We're here on another matter."

"You are the police though, right?" Mrs. Davis asked.

"Of a sort, yes," Marcus answered. Dominic cut his eyes at him—just long enough to make sure he got the message—and then turned to the woman.

"Yes, we are police ma'am. And we are here on a police matter." He pulled a folded document from his pocket and held it up. "In fact, I have a warrant to search the premises."

Dr. Davis stood up straight then, and leaned toward Dominic in the way a man who is used to getting his way through years of privilege might. "Well," he said, and when he did, he drew the word out into a long, disapproving sigh, "I'm not sure if you know who I am, but it's not just the Chief of Police I play golf with."

"Oh I'm not here to learn about your athletic endeavors, sir. The fact is I know plenty about who you've played golf with. Including Monsignor Stiles."

The look of ironclad assurance on Davis's face cracked a bit.

Dominic grinned. "Oh, I see that you know what this is about now, don't you? You figured it out."

Suddenly Dr. Davis didn't seem so intimidating.

"Whatever happened to the Monsignor?" Dominic said, taking a step toward the doctor and forcing him back. "Oh that's right, he was arrested, wasn't he? Something about domestic terrorism. You know, we never did nail down all his accomplices."

"Sir, please!" Mrs. Davis cried. The nervous laughter that followed almost hurt Marcus's ears. "Let's not fight."

"No, Mrs. Davis, there's no need to fight. We have a valid search warrant here, which means there's nothing to fight about. But I want you to know that we can be very reasonable men. Right, Marcus?" He turned to the other man but didn't really acknowledge him. "We don't want to put you two out any longer than we have to. So why don't you just give up the girl?"

Dr. Davis said the same thing every guilty man ever has. "Girl? I'm afraid I don't know what you are talking about."

"Hmmm." Dominic pursed his lips as if he was considering the truthfulness of the doctor's statement before turning away from the man and walking to the end of the kitchen island. "The thing is, doctor," he said, before facing him again, "you do. We all know you do. She knows. My partner here knows. You and I, we aren't fools. We both know, too. I guess we could tear your house apart. I could call in a dozen agents. Open every drawer, including the one Mrs. Davis has next to the bed upstairs. No telling what we might find there. We might even stumble upon some drugs, a gun, something else illegal. Something you might not even know is around here."

"I'm not some kid on the street," Dr. Davis said, "You can't threaten me and think you'll get away with it."

"No, I know plenty of street kids. They don't have anywhere near as much to lose as you do, doctor." Dominic put his hand on the doctor's shoulder and implored him in the way a good friend might ask another to do the right thing. "Just give us the girl."

Davis stood there, the defiance returning in full strength. He said nothing.

Dominic sighed. "All right. Fine. But honestly, I don't need your help. I know exactly where she is." A sheen of true fear spread across the doctor's face. "You told me the moment we walked in the door."

Mrs. Davis was on the edge of tears. "What?" she gasped. Dominic ignored her.

"Marcus, the pantry. There'll be a latch in there somewhere that should open up a hidden compartment."

"Now wait just a minute . . ."

Dominic stepped forward and in one fluid motion unholstered his weapon before jamming the barrel of the gun directly underneath the doctor's chin.

"I've heard just about enough from you." He jerked his head to the left. "Now get over there with your wife. She needs you."

For a moment, no one moved, but then the doctor slipped away from Dominic, wrapping his arms around his wife who was now in full hysterics. Dominic turned to Marcus, who still hadn't taken a step. His voice was calm, cold, and clinical.

"All right, Marcus. Do it."

Marcus eyed the pantry door. He took a cautious step toward it, then another. When he opened the door, he half expected the girl to come flying out, gun or knife in hand. But there was nothing but a cupboard filled with canned foods and dried goods. For a second, Marcus even wondered if Dominic was wrong.

But then he heard a sniffle, followed by an intake of breath, sharp and sudden. She was in there somewhere. Hiding. He felt around the inside of the door, hands searching for a switch or a button or a latch. He only knew he'd found it when the rear wall slid away so fast that he jumped back in shock. And there, lying in a tiny crawlspace barely big enough to fit her, was a girl who couldn't have been older than twenty.

From behind him, Dominic said:

"Jackpot."

Chapter 11

In the weeks that followed A-Day, what the United States had been—its essence, its soul, its sense of destiny—melted away. The physical damage was horrible, but the spiritual wound was deadly. Oh, there was the normal wellspring of patriotism, the rallying to the cause. Blood and money was given. Men and women joined the armed forces because they didn't know what else to do. Marcus had been one of them.

But there was no one to fight. No one to revenge against. The war, the deadliest in world history, had lasted all of an hour.

Marcus didn't go to boot camp; not at first, at least. He was sent west the day after he signed his papers, stationed in Denver as part of the force tasked with restoring power and the rule of law—usually in that order—to the millions who were without both.

He was glad he never went any farther, was never assigned to the units whose uniform consisted of full-body radiation suits, even if he was curious to see what had become of the great cities of the West. The men and women who went to the coast weren't the same when they came back.

They had seen what could not be unseen.

Most of them tried to hide it, to act as though they were too tough, too experienced, to do anything other than move on. They could not hide their eyes though, the haunted look that marked them.

No, Marcus never went west. He never saw the burned-out cities, the charred bodies, the shadows of men, women, and children who had been vaporized. He would see much worse—and do much worse—before his days of service were over.

* * *

The girl was lying on the ground whimpering, curled up into a tight ball. She would have disappeared into herself if it were possible. That much was clear. She had pressed against the wall and was still trying to crawl even further into the corner, but there was nowhere to go. Marcus stood over her, gawking.

Dominic pulled out his DNA scanner and took a reading. "Rachel Carson," he said. "She's a runner.

"Miss Carson, it is my duty under the Rostov Protocol of 26 U.S.C. section 5001 to inform you that you are carrying a Class 1 undesirable which we are required to terminate."

"God no. Please don't."

Marcus turned and looked at Mrs. Davis. She was pleading with him, struggling against her husband who held her tight, begging Marcus not to do something. In that moment, he wasn't even sure what.

"Marcus," Dominic said, "it's time."

Marcus turned and looked dumbly at Dominic. It was only when he saw the small gun that Dominic was holding out to him, with its cruel lines and sharp points, that he realized what was happening. This was his test, his price of admission.

He looked from the gun to the girl and back again. Dominic gestured to him with the weapon, never taking his eyes off him. "You can do this," he said.

Marcus made his decision. He took a step toward Dominic and reached out to take the Spiker. The Davis woman screamed out again, but Marcus no longer heard her.

"You just pull the slide on the side. You'll feel the charge. Then you just point . . . and shoot. You got it?"

Marcus felt the weight of the gun in his hand. It was heavier than he thought it would be. He ran his fingers along the two metal prongs all the way to the point.

"Yeah. I got it."

He turned to the girl who was still cowering in the crawl space behind the closet. She didn't look pregnant, and she probably wasn't that far along. The Davises were standing behind him, the doctor holding his wife tight against him as she cried into his chest. The girl was looking at Marcus now, her frightened eyes pleading with him. Yet there was resignation there too. She knew what he was here to do, and she knew that he would do it.

He raised his weapon. The girl started scrambling again, trying to somehow force her body to become one with the wall. Marcus pulled the slide back on the gun. And he did feel the charge. He felt the power in his hand. The girl stopped struggling, but she didn't stop looking at Marcus. She would make him look her in the eyes when he did this.

"I'm sorry."

Marcus pulled the trigger.

There was a whine, a high-pitched tone. The two parallel prongs of the gun glowed blue for a moment before a bolt of energy erupted from the end. It struck the girl before him, and Marcus could have sworn that he saw it in her eyes the moment the life inside of her faded away. She stopped struggling. Stopped crying. It was over. She would mourn later.

Marcus didn't notice Dominic standing next to him until he clapped a hand down on his shoulder. "Good job," he said. "Miss Carson, you're going to want to go to the hospital tomorrow."

Dominic removed a card from his chest pocket. "You'll want to give them this card," he said, taking a step toward her, "and they'll check you out. No cost, no questions. But first . . ." Dominic pulled his sidearm and aimed it at the girl's head. Marcus stood there in shock, but did not react. "I'd like you to remove the knife you are hiding behind you and throw it on the floor in front of me."

The girl's eyes locked on Dominic, full of hatred. Then she grinned, a mirthless, soulless smile. She reached behind her and pulled out a kitchen knife. She held it up in the air and tossed it in front of Dominic. It fell to the ground with a hollow clatter.

Dominic kicked it away, then turned to Davis, who was still holding his wife, staring dumbly at the girl in the pantry. Dominic smiled, but it was more like a sneer. "Tools of the trade, huh? You teach them all to use a knife? A doctor knows where to cut, right? So they'll bleed out quick?"

"I wouldn't know what you're talking about."

"No," Dominic said, finally lowering his gun. "I guess you wouldn't." Then he took a step toward the girl and threw the card down on her chest. "Go to the doctor. Get checked out. Forget this ever happened, forget these people, and move on."

Dominic reached out and took the Spiker from Marcus's hand. "Let's go. And you two," he said, pointing at the Davises with his gun, "normally I'd burn this place to the ground, preferably with you both in it. But it seems, Dr. Davis, that you play golf with the right people after all. But if I show up on your doorstep again, things will be different. You got me?"

Davis didn't flinch. "Yeah," he said, "we got you." The two men stared across a gulf of a couple of feet at each other, and Marcus wondered if Dominic might just shoot the man, connections be damned. Instead, Dominic slid his gun back in his holster, and he and Marcus left the house behind.

Chapter 12

Nothing but the *harump, harump, harump* of the car on old roads broke the silence as they drove back to DC. Dominic was lost in his own thoughts, more so than Marcus had seen him in the short time they had known each other. Not that he cared. Marcus didn't much feel like talking either.

He had killed before, during the war. And not only from a distance. He'd done it up close, face-to-face. He'd felt the life drain out of another person, seen as the light fled their eyes. Funny thing about that light. He'd heard people talk about it, of course. Everyone from poets to characters in movies to his own father who had fancied himself a bit of a romantic. And yet Marcus had never seen that light, not really. Not until he looked in the eyes of someone as the light was extinguished. As *he* extinguished it. Then he saw. Then he knew.

He'd seen it again today, in the girl's eyes. He'd seen it dim when he fired the Spiker. Not extinguished. But it would never burn as bright. It didn't matter what came after. How happy she was, or how many Clear children she had. Something was lost, something had died. And there was no bringing it back.

They pulled into the parking lot of the supposedly abandoned factory building. Dominic drove around back to the area where Marcus's car was hidden. He stopped beside it and put the car in park, but he didn't turn off the ignition. Instead, he turned to Marcus and said, "You did good today. Couldn't have done better, in fact. There's nothing more I could have asked of you."

Marcus just nodded. "Thanks," he muttered.

"I know it's not easy. I wish I could tell you it gets better, but this is not that kind of game.

"It's always the same. They run until they can't run anymore, then they hide, and we find them. It's always us and them. They've got their backs against some wall in an alley or in an abandoned building or whatever, and the only escape is behind us. Still, they almost never fight. Most of them are in no condition to, anyway. But even the ones who could, don't. There's a kind of acceptance that comes over a person, when you've done all you can and there's nothing left to do.

"People always say they'll go down fighting. That they'll never give up. But in the end, they do. I saw it time and again during the war. Rows and rows of people. On their knees. Bullet to the back of the head. All in a line. All in a perfect damn line. I always wondered—why don't they run? Why don't they at least try to get away? It used to kill me, thinking about that. I just couldn't stop, you know? I thought about it every time I saw them. I thought about it every damn day. I don't anymore."

Marcus listened, but if Dominic's words were meant to help, they missed their mark. All he could see was that pleading in the girl's eyes, that fading light.

"How do you do it, then?" Marcus asked. "If it doesn't get easier? How do you keep making that call?"

Dominic breathed deep, and let it all out in a long sigh. "You have to believe with all your heart that what we are doing is the right thing. You have to imagine what the world would be like if we didn't do it."

"And what is that?"

"Hell," Dominic said, staring straight out into the coming twilight. "It would be chaos again. Lawlessness. Death. All the bad people in the world returned from the grave. Like zombies, like in all those movies before the war. Come back and want nothing but to take another pound of flesh from society. Irredeemable, with no purpose but to do harm. Like the Ashkhani."

Marcus shivered at the sound of their name. "The Ashkhani had a choice," he said. "They made a decision to serve Khan. I don't think you can say the same of the Reborn."

"They made their choice, too," Dominic said. "The Reborn. Whenever it was, they made it, and if you gave them the chance, they'd make it again.

"The Ashkhani are all the proof you'll ever need. Some men are born evil, and they just spend their lives looking for an outlet. Society couldn't create the Ashkhani, not alone. Khan saw it in them, better than any DNA test ever could. People like you and me, we could never have been Ashkhani. We could never have been a part of that cult. No, people are like any other animal. Some of them are diseased from the start, and there's no curing them.

"And that leaves you with only one choice."

Chapter 13

The Ashkhani stepped from the nightmares of ten centuries. They came to a world that did not know them and could not conceive of them. A soft world, unprepared for the reaping.

Marcus had been in Colorado for six months, helping to restore some semblance of order, some veneer of civilization to places that had fallen into anarchy and chaos. Marcus had never thought about how fragile, how delicate the thin web of civil society could be, or how easy it could collapse upon itself. Electricity was the fire of the modern world, and without it, the darkness ruled all.

The EMP shockwave had fried high-voltage transformers for a thousand miles in every direction. The backbone of the western grid was broken, and it could not be easily fixed. That meant no power, which meant no water from central waterworks, and no gasoline from electric gas pumps. That was only the beginning. Everything with a computer chip—every phone, every appliance, every car, every GPS unit, every watch, coffee maker, and baby monitor—became useless.

Thus when it came to fuel and food, the army couldn't live off the land. Supply chains had to be created. Everything from spare parts to water had to be shipped in from the East, by truck, rail, and airplane. And meanwhile, millions waited. They waited in cities and towns, in farmhouses and gated communities. They waited for food, for gas, for basic medicines.

Then they began to starve.

Then they began to fight, and to maim, and to kill.

When the water and the food ran out, four thousand years of culture, of religion, of morality, of civilization, burned away like morning dew on a summer day.

Marcus didn't want to know how many died in the months and years that followed. He didn't like to think about it. Rumors persisted in the West that order never was restored to some places, that there were little villages and towns in the high mountains or in the deep desert that were still wild places where the gun was the law.

And yet as bad as those days were, they could not compare to the chaos that came after the broadcast, when the Ashkhani arose.

* * *

Marcus drove home as dusk settled over Washington. He guided his car through the narrow streets of Georgetown toward the apartment that he had to himself. It was a place he could never have afforded before the war. But DC was different now. The government had done something no one would have ever imagined thirty years before—it had shrunk. There wasn't as much money to support it, and there wasn't as much need for it anyway.

The country was breaking. He could feel it. He wasn't sure when the division would finally come, but it was only a matter of time. Hawaii had never come back, even after the Ashkhani who had captured it were finally eradicated. Alaska had been on its own throughout the duration of the war, and in that time the independence movement had finally grown strong enough to dominate the state's government. The Supreme Court had ruled the state's act of succession illegal, but the Alaskans had simply ignored it. A federal judge who tried to enforce the Court's order was expelled, dropped off at a border crossing in the Yukon and told never to return. With the Southern Union, unofficial though it might be, Marcus couldn't help but believe the end was near.

Something of the American spirit had died on A-Day, and whatever strength was left to bring it back was used up in the war that followed. The broadcast was the beginning.

It was two years after A-Day, and the Khitan Khanate, as China was then called, had been busy. The cult of Khan had spread from China on the winds of his voice, preached by missionaries who were sent into the world, teaching of the fulfilled prophesy of Khan's return. Mongolia had fallen first of its own volition. The government of Ulaanbaatar had come to Luoyang and pledged its undying loyalty to Khan. Burma followed, then Bhutan and Bangladesh, all without a shot being fired. It was the force of personality that brought them, the promise of a future of purpose—along with an absolute surety that Khan would take them by force otherwise.

It was remarkable, but the nations of the earth took little notice, not until Southeast Asia fell like dominos—Laos, Cambodia, Vietnam, and Thailand became vassal states of the Khanate. If that made the leaders of the world sit up and take notice, they fell out of their chairs when the Korean Union pledged fealty to Khitan. Malaysia and Indonesia followed as a fait accompli. When India presented Khan with the sacred lotus flower, the emblem of Indian royalty, the Khitan Khanate could count half the world's population as under its rule.

But not everyone was so willing to bow their knee to Khan.

To Japan, Khan delivered a message espousing that all nations were members of one family, and that a family could have only one father. To that, in the rarest of public declarations, the Japanese Emperor responded directly, saying only, "He who would build his home upon the shifting sands of pride should beware the divine wind." Russia was even more direct. From the Kremlin—"We have faced you before. We will face you again. And you will die before you ever see the spires of Moscow."

The world hung on a knife's edge, and all wondered which way it would fall.

It was then that Khan spoke the nations into chaos.

The broadcast began with static. Marcus was on leave that week, having gone to Chicago for much needed rest and relaxation. He was walking down the street they called the Golden Mile when every television in every store window went blank, when every radio station on the air went silent.

Marcus noticed. They all did. Everyone had been on edge for too long, and their senses were heightened. So when the silence came, they all stopped. People walking down the streets. People in their cars. People in their offices. They stopped, and they fiddled with radios and televisions and the few internet streams that still functioned. And then a piercing tone burst through the air, followed by a voice that spoke in perfect English, tinted only slightly by the accent of a foreign land—

I am the all-father. Today, I speak to the people. I do not address myself to the leaders of this world, to the parasites that feed on their slaves, that drug the nations with the opiate of democracy, with the lie of the vote. No, I have no words for them. To them I wish only ignominy, only failure, only loss, only hard justice and the sentence that all deserve who kill, who enslave. The same punishment as is meted out to the pirate, the enemy of the world, hostis humani generis.

I speak to the ones who struggle, the ones who strive. I call to the downtrodden, to the poor, to the forgotten. I have not forgotten you. Nor do I forget those who are rich in goods but poor in spirit. You who have conquered hunger and want, only to become slaves to the crushing weight of expectations. You wallow in fear. You pass the days until your death. Your life is pointless.

To you, I say—lay down your burdens. Let go your fears. Forget the ties of the past, the chains of your mistakes, the shackles of your decisions.

Come, and I will gather you to me, my children.

I will give you life. I will give you freedom. Not the pointless illusion of democracy, but the true liberty of serving a cause greater than yourself. You come to me on your knees. I will give you my hand.

And then you will rise.

But freedom comes with a price. You have sinned. Sinned against yourself, and sinned against your fellow man. You have built the rotten empire of your life on the corpses of others. Your sins are great, and the dead cry out for vengeance. You must atone.

I am the scourge of the Lord. I am the punishment of God. And the Ashkhani are my whip . . .

The voice went silent, the sound of crackling static replacing it. For a moment Marcus heard nothing. He stood there, in the middle of the street, surrounded by so many others doing the same.

And then the wail.

That was how Marcus always described it—a wail. But even that didn't do it justice. He called it that because of a movie he had seen when he was young, the story of a demon, a banshee, that drove men mad and stole their souls with her mind-rending shriek. It was the closest thing he could compare it to. But it was so much worse than that. It could not truly be described.

Only experienced.

Marcus turned to see where that hell-blast came from, and at first he thought he had gone mad himself. There was a woman thirty feet away. She was standing in the middle of the road. She looked like all of them, just another cog in the machine, another lawyer or businesswoman dressed in gray slacks and a matching jacket over a white blouse. Five foot three and maybe a hundred and twenty pounds at the most. And yet she roared, her head thrown back, her voice echoing through the streets so loudly that Marcus wondered if her vocal cords would be shredded, if blood would pour from her mouth when she was finished.

Other cries joined hers, one after another, like wolves howling at a bitter moon from all around him, and Marcus suddenly knew real fear. A worker on the street corner in a hardhat, a twenty-something in running gear, a man who had been playing Frisbee with a dog only a few minutes before, a mother with a baby stroller—all of them, crying out with a voice that could turn water to ice. Marcus and the others remained rooted in place, held fast by the sound. Staring. Unable to move. Unable to react.

Then the first woman stopped.

She lowered her gaze and Marcus saw in her eyes a singularity of purpose, a raging hate he had never before witnessed. She marched over to another woman who was paralyzed with shock, reaching inside her own jacket and pulling out a short, curved blade. With one swift movement she slit the woman's throat, nearly decapitating her. The victim collapsed to the ground while her murderer bathed in her blood.

Then, chaos.

People screamed and ran like sheep before the slaughter. Marcus stumbled backwards into the wall of a drugstore. He watched as the man in the hardhat hacked a young boy to death. The mother had removed a blade from her stroller and was chasing a man in a business suit across the street. The man's dog had leapt on the back of a cyclist, dragging him to the ground where his master finished him off. Two people went crashing through a window five stories up in the building across from Marcus, smashing into the roof of a parked car, setting its alarm blaring. In the store behind him, a cashier had leapt over the counter and decapitated a woman in front of her daughter. She was still holding the young girl's hand as she toppled over.

The woman in the tight spandex and sports bra ripped her iPod from her ears and threw it aside. She walked over to a trash can and pulled a machete from behind it. She locked eyes on Marcus and started toward him. Slow at first, and then breaking into a run, arms and legs pumping up and down in time, the blade of the machete glimmering in the summer sun. She was almost upon him when a shot rang out and her head exploded. Her momentum carried her forward, and she collapsed in a bloody splash before Marcus's feet.

He looked down at his service weapon, gazing at the 9 mm as if he'd never seen anything like it before. Something clicked in his head, and he went to work.

He shot the woman in the business suit first, before turning to the man in the hardhat and putting two rounds in his chest. He told the woman with the baby to stop, but when she came at him with her blade, he had no choice but to put her down. He killed the dog just as it ripped the throat out of someone in the park and then killed its master. He shot the clerk in the drugstore through the plateglass window, but not before she gutted the little girl cowering next to her dead mother's body. He had seven rounds left, and judging from the terrified howls that echoed down the streets of Chicago, that wouldn't be nearly enough.

Marcus ran. He had no plans, he had no idea where he'd go. He thought about finding a place to hide, but something told him that was a mistake. He had to get out of the city. Screams, gunshots, explosions seemed to surround him. He ducked into an alley, slipping between buildings, trying to escape the chaos. He was about to emerge on one of the main roads when he stopped, throwing himself into a doorway where he hoped no one could see him.

A group of them were moving down the street, their blades gleaming. Marcus watched as they came upon a wounded man. He begged for mercy, but without a word a woman in a black business suit plunged a knife into his throat. They moved on, searching for others.

Marcus had just stepped out of the shadow of the alleyway when a police car came screaming down the street, spinning around to miss the body of one of the women lying dead on the pavement. It had barely come to a halt when two cops leapt out, drawing their guns and pointing them at Marcus.

"You one of them?" the driver, a big man whose shirt was stained with fresh sweat, screamed.

Marcus held up his gun. "I think they prefer knives," he said.

The cops looked around at the bodies on the ground, long bladed weapons lying next to some of them. The wounded moaned and cried out for help, but the police ignored them.

The officer lowered his weapon. "You a cop?"

"Army."

"Based on what we got on the radio, we're going to need you. The whole city's gone crazy."

"But more police are on their way, right?"

The two cops looked at each other. The one on the far side of the car shook his head. "What we've got left will come. Whatever this is, it got some of us, too."

"We killed four beat cops before we came down here. One of them I'd known for years. He just snapped, like the rest of them. Now the 9th Precinct's been overrun. We barely made it out alive. Figured we'd regroup and hit back once we knew what the hell is going on here."

"It was the broadcast," Marcus said. "That's what triggered it."

Someone screamed in the distance as a man went running down the road, sprinting past them. Marcus turned and shot the woman following him, a teenage girl in a floral print skirt. She went flying to the ground, the knife she carried clattering along the asphalt.

"Sweet Jesus." The cop stumbled back toward the driver's side of his cruiser. "If you're coming, let's go!"

Marcus nodded and ran over to where they waited. He was just climbing inside when a roar echoed through the skyscraper-walled canyons of the city. They all looked up as a 747 curled above them, plummeting toward the ground. They watched as it spun in the air, turning in a slow death spiral until it was upside-down. It disappeared over the false horizon of the city, but only a handful of seconds later there was an explosion that shook the earth and sent a column of flame into the sky.

They stared up at the fire longer than they should have before Marcus finally said, "We should get out of the city."

The big cop looked at Marcus with terror in his eyes. "Yeah," he said. "Yeah."

They climbed into the car and sped away, leaving the wounded and dying behind.

Chapter 14

Marcus sat in his car, parked in front of his apartment, a thousand miles and two decades from that day in Chicago. And yet he could still feel the fear, still smell the blood and the death.

They had fled the city, driving as fast as they could, taking the sidewalks or the parks when abandoned cars or flaming wreckage blocked their way. They slowed down only when they passed one of what they would later learn were the Ashkhani, shooting them dead where they found them. They made no effort to subdue them, no effort to contain them, to read them their rights, or arrest them. Somehow they knew that that way of doing things was over, that those quaint notions no longer had a place in this world. This was total war, anyone could be the enemy, and it was kill or be killed.

They stopped bothering to fight back when they came upon a rogue SWAT team that had surrounded four cops who were bunkered in behind a burning car. The other Ashkhani ran free behind the well-armed death squad, finishing off anyone who had survived their initial onslaught. Marcus looked down at his 9 mm, sliding out the clip. It was empty. The cop in the driver's seat caught his eye in the rearview mirror. Marcus shook his head. They didn't try and help.

They drove until they reached the outskirts of the city, where Marcus thanked his God above that a National Guard unit was organizing. Whatever had happened in Chicago, there was still order beyond it. But the truth was far worse than he could have imagined.

The commander of the Guard unit was a captain as green as they came, a weekend warrior who wanted to serve his country and help his fellow citizens, never imagining that those same people would one day try and kill him. When he met Marcus and found out he was an honest-to-God soldier, he promptly told him far more than he should have.

"It's happening everywhere," he said as dark clouds of smoke began to gather over Chicago.

"Everywhere? All of Illinois?"

"No! Everywhere. All over the country. Maybe all over the world."

Marcus was staggered. He'd figured as much, but it hadn't hit home until he heard it confirmed.

"But the military is unaffected?"

"I wouldn't say that," the man said. "I heard they had to put some guys down at Peoria, but yeah more or less. For now at least it seems like it's mostly the civilian population. The last I heard, any outbreaks in the military were contained."

Outbreaks. He was talking about it like it was a disease. And maybe it was. A disease of the mind and the soul, far more dangerous than those of the body.

"Still, it will take some time for them to mobilize."

"What are your orders?"

The man's eyes clouded with fear. "We are supposed to establish a base of operations here. And then reconnoiter the city and see how bad things are."

"Things are bad. You don't have to go in there to see that."

"Yeah," the man said, his voice quivering, "but orders are orders, right?"

Two hours later, the captain led a convoy of armored vehicles back toward Chicago. Marcus never saw him again.

In the end, Chicago was lost on that day, the day of what many came to call The Rising. The captain had been right; the same nightmare had played out in cities around the country, and in countries around the world. In some places—Chicago, Detroit, Cleveland, Pittsburgh, Hawaii, and parts of the states of Michigan, Wisconsin, Ohio, Pennsylvania, New York, and Vermont—the

Ashkhani had secretly spread so far through the ranks of the police and the populace that they were simply too entrenched to be overcome. The same happened throughout the powerless West, where hunger and hardship had plowed the fields for the seeds of rebellion and revolution to flourish. But those uprisings were quickly quashed by military units already in place to provide humanitarian relief. The transition from peacekeeper to warrior was swift, and the death toll was staggering. But the damage could not be measured in human lives alone.

Even though the Ashkhani were wiped out in the continental US early in the war, the specter of their potential return hung over the people. They weren't like enemies of the past. Americans weren't "all in it together." Neighbor looked on neighbor with suspicion. Friends no longer trusted one another. Even the closest family member was suspect.

The Ashkhani hadn't been invaders. They weren't some "other" that could be demonized. They could be anyone, anyone at all.

The natural assumption was that more Ashkhani were waiting, plotting another rising. That deep-cover agents of the Khan lived in every neighborhood, in every state. And that one day, just as they had come before, they would return.

But the Ashkhani would never rise again.

At least not officially. Rumors persisted of towns that suddenly went off the grid. They were always just big enough to notice, but not big enough to matter. They had names like Jackson, West Virginia; Fisher's Gap, Ohio; and Priory, Montana. Some people began to whisper about government fire teams who were charged with making such places disappear, lest the Ashkhani's attacks disrupt the nation's morale. The truth of the matter was never quite clear.

In fact, many things remained a mystery. Social scientists and philosophers would debate for years why certain places fell to the Ashkhani while others did not. Why New York City and Boston smashed the uprising while Chicago and Detroit succumbed. Why the South and Midwest were almost entirely unaffected, and the Great Lakes region became overwhelmed.

The same questions could be asked around the world. South America and Africa bowed to the Khan, while Mexico's drug cartels put aside their blood feuds to fight against *Los Poseídos*. Across the ocean, the Islamic World came together to repel the Infidels, while Europe was divided. France, Germany, Italy, Spain, and the nations that surrounded them quickly capitulated. It wasn't that the numbers of Ashkhani were great there. The peoples of Central Europe were tired; they simply lacked the will to resist. And thus, the British were left alone again. The Gallic Protocol was activated, the Chunnel flooded, and England prepared itself for yet another long siege. Eastern Europe turned to the Russians for help, and they were more than eager to give it—for a price, of course.

On the same day the Ashkhani appeared, Khan and his horde invaded southern Russia, while their bombers struck Tokyo, Osaka, and Nagasaki. In the skies above, the Chāoxīnxīng—China's orbital hunter-killers—were activated. Within hours, seventy-five percent of the world's satellites had been destroyed, with the debris field they created taking the rest. In the dark nights that were to come, Marcus would often look up from the Mongolian steppe and admire the beauty of a million points of light that held sway in the evening sky, shining brighter than the stars. They were his lone comfort in those days, even if they represented everything he was fighting against.

For the war had begun. Before it was over, nearly two-thirds of the world's population would be dead.

Chapter 15

Marcus slept that night, but not peacefully. His dreams jumped from one nightmare to another, some things he'd seen, others he'd only heard of. The Battle of Vladivostok, the linchpin to the entire invasion of Asia. In his dreams he was there again, in that corpse city. The Ashkhani had turned it into one great booby trap. Every building was rigged to blow, each body laced with trip wires, mines around every corner.

They'd lost thousands in that frozen city, and Marcus had seen more than one man ripped apart before his very eyes. Nothing left but a fine pink mist that stuck in his throat and coated the inside of his mouth. And then the long march from Vladivostok into the Chinese interior, the roads paved with their own dead as the tip of the spear pierced into the heart of Khan's empire.

When the fighting began, they were told that they would win the war, and then they would win the peace. That the war would be total, but that they would rebuild. Marcus had believed it. But the rivers of blood they unleashed seemed as if they might wash the earth clean of life. There were no civilians, no innocents, no noncombatants. The world had gone mad, and it could not be cured.

The march ended at the hills above Luoyang, ten miles from the capital, the last bastion of Khan's power, the place where he would make his stand. They would grind the city into dust. They would bring its walls down around him. The city would be his tomb. Marcus had been there.

The Ashkhani had darkened the buildings, and only the near-constant flashes of lightning illuminated the doomed city below. The rain came in torrents, pouring off Marcus's greatcoat, soaking him despite the waterproof clothing he wore. The only other time he'd seen it rain like this was the summer before his father died, on a lake in Alabama, when the heavens had opened up and he'd had to bail out the boat with his hat as his father steered them back to the shore. It was one of the few happy memories he had of the man.

Marcus held a stopwatch, the seconds ticking down instead of up. He gazed upon the formation of the big 250s, as lightning flashed off the polished steel of the great guns' barrels. Two hours before, he had been temporarily reassigned to the artillery. The generals wanted to send a signal. They wanted to harness the thunder, to bring down the lightning. And so Marcus stood, watching as the seconds counted down, until they reached zero, and then the fifty thousand guns of the American Expeditionary Force would open up, as one.

Down the clock ran, and with every second the night seemed to grow darker. At thirty seconds, Marcus lit his flare. Along the Hen Lei Heights the tiny lights burst forth in the night, fifty thousand fireflies fighting against the darkness. When the clock hit ten, Marcus held the flare high above his head. The night went silent. The wind died away. The storm held its breath. 5, 4, 3, 2. When the clock hit one, Marcus waited a half-beat and dropped his arm. The world awoke to sound and fury.

Fifty thousand guns belched flame and terror. Such was the force of the blast that Marcus was thrown to the ground. The 250s fired free now, hurling bombs down on the city below as quickly as their crews could reload them. Marcus pushed himself up from the mud to a night gone mad. They sky glowed red like it might split apart and pour down the end of the earth. Each burst shook Marcus to his core, each shot like a punch to the gut. Fire and steel filled the air, and with each second that passed, hundreds, if not thousands, died in the necropolis below. Marcus had become Death, the destroyer of worlds.

That was what Marcus saw in his dreams that night, as he had so many times before. But for the first time in a long time, his dream was different. For he saw something else, as well. Rachel Carson's pale blue eyes, the pleading look, and then the hatred. Her eyes seemed to hang over it all.

* * *

His phone woke him. He didn't recognize the number, but the voice was unmistakable.

"Get up," Dominic said. "We've got a problem."

Fifteen minutes later, Marcus was guiding his car through the abandoned streets of Northwest Washington, past the new wilderness of the old Rock Creek Park to Brightwood. He wondered if he'd be able to find his destination even with the map he kept in the glove compartment, the luxury of the old GPS systems a distant memory. He stopped worrying when he saw the column of black smoke soaring into the sky, backlit by the rising sun.

He stopped the car in front of a city police cordon, something he'd never seen in his entire time on the force. He climbed out and recognized Mike Haidet, one of the cops from his old precinct, pacing nervously along the perimeter. Haidet stepped forward with his hand out. "I'm sorry sir, but this is a restricted area." His voice was quivering. Whatever had happened was beyond his capability to process.

"Haidet, it's me. Marcus. Marcus Ryder."

Haidet gawked at him like he hadn't seen him in ages.

"Marcus? What the hell are you doing here, man? You're retired!"

Marcus didn't bother trying to keep a straight face at that euphemism, so earnestly uttered.

"Yeah. I've got a new job now. What happened here, Mike?"

Sweat broke out along the man's brow. "Oh man. I've never seen anything like it. I've heard stories from the war. But that's about as close as I can get."

An explosion ripped through the morning sky, and another ball of black smoke surged into the air, joining the greater column.

Haidet gazed up at the acrid plume and shook his head. "There are bodies," he said. "Everywhere. But it don't make no sense, you know? There's nobody out here. I always thought this whole area was abandoned."

Marcus started walking toward the source of the last explosion, and Haidet fell in beside him, no longer bothering to ask him questions about why he was there.

"What happened?"

"Gas explosion. Or at least, that's what the fed in charge said. Big, mean looking guy."

Marcus grinned again. "I'm sure it's fine."

"I guess. I guess it's possible one of the mains broke. But still, none of it makes sense. All those people here, in an abandoned factory? And then a gas explosion, in a place that hasn't had a tenant in over a decade? Why was the gas even still on, you know?"

Marcus stopped and put an arm around the other man, younger in years and so much more so in experience. "Sometimes, it's better not to ask questions. Not everything's going to make sense. Why don't you wait here and I'll go see what I can find out?" He slapped Haidet on the back and left him standing there, more confused than when Marcus arrived.

Haidet had been right about the devastation. Whatever had stood there once was long gone now, ripped apart by an explosion of some magnitude. Marcus had seen a gas line blow before, right after he'd come back to DC and joined the police force. He knew what damage they could do, and what he saw now was consistent. The building had been disintegrated, debris strewn about the perimeter, all of it either aflame or charred beyond recognition. He couldn't yet see the source of the fire when the smell hit him.

Once again, Haidet had nailed it; it was just like the war. The odor of burning flesh mingled with the unmistakable stench of death. He passed a couple paramedics, standing with their hands on their hips, their faces slack with boredom. Even in this new, better world, people still died. These men had seen it before, in all its forms, in all its guises. This did not faze them.

Marcus followed their eyes to the pit a hundred feet away, fire leaping from its open maw like it was a gateway to Hell. Bodies—what was left of them—were everywhere, too many to try and cover. Even as Marcus looked over them, he felt nothing, and somewhere inside he longed for the innocence of Officer Mike Haidet.

He didn't think on it long, though, not once he recognized the man standing on the edge of the descent, his hands stuffed in his pockets, a cigarette dangling from his lips.

"I was wondering when you'd get here," Dominic said as Marcus stopped beside him. He flicked his cigarette into the chasm and whistled, long and low. "Ever seen anything like it?"

Marcus leaned forward and gazed into the pit. "Not for a long time," he said.

"Me neither."

"I heard it was a gas main explosion."

"Who told you that?"

"Cop on the perimeter. I assume he's mistaken."

"No, it's a gas main all right. That's the story we'll tell the press. It helps that it's true. Somewhat at least. Someone placed Semtex along the gas line that ran beneath this building. And along the structural supports of the foundation, the sub-basement, the works. I guess they thought the gas would cover their tracks. Or maybe they didn't care. I'm not sure anymore."

Dominic pulled a pack of cigarettes from his pocket and, after removing one, offered them to Marcus. He declined.

"Didn't know you smoked."

"We've been partners for a day," Dominic said. He took a long drag and arched his back, blowing the smoke so that it joined the plume that still poured from the open pit before them. "There are a lot of things you don't know about me."

"I take it this was not an abandoned warehouse."

Dominic had already finished half his cigarette. "No," he said, "it was not."

"One of ours?"

"Yeah. One of ours."

A fire crew had arrived, and they were pouring a steady stream of water down into the depths of the opening in front of them. Their efforts seemed to have little effect. Marcus figured they would be there all day and maybe into the night.

Dominic was pensive. Worried. It was not what Marcus was used to, even if Dominic was right that he didn't really know him. Whatever had happened at the abandoned factory the night before had shaken him.

A helicopter flew overhead, its light shining down on the two men and what remained of the warehouse. The logo on the side said it was from one of the local news stations.

"Won't be able to keep this one out of the press," Marcus said.

"They'll be happy enough with the excuse. It still makes a good story. You and me though, we got work to do." Dominic gestured at the open pit. "I guess if you did the same thing to our shop, this is what it would look like."

A chill rippled through Marcus. On some level, he knew the job was dangerous. Certainly more so than the one he'd just left. But he hadn't considered he might get killed. "You mean this was a field office?"

Dominic nodded. "We don't normally have two in one city. In fact, most of them cover a pretty wide area. We're understaffed, you know. But this one had a very special purpose. Congress, when they passed Warren-Rostov, insisted on one thing—they wanted all the info centralized. Claimed it was a privacy issue. I always figured they wanted control, you know? As long as they got the data, nobody can screw with them. Anyway, we keep everything, everything that makes this possible, all our files, all our DNA records, on two servers. One of them is in the lowest level of HQ. The other one . . ." Dominic gestured at the open pit with his cigarette. "Something tells me we won't recover it."

"But who has the capability to do something like this?"

Dominic crushed out his cigarette and shrugged his shoulders. "Nobody, I thought. Most of the groups we deal with are doing one-off shit. Religious types, activists. They stay in the shadows, ferrying runners down South. The ones who run the clinics can be more dangerous, but you know that from experience. This is something different. This took a lot of intelligence, a lot of planning. Not to mention some heavy artillery, and a lot of men. It worries me, to tell you the truth. If they found this place, they'll find HQ. That will be their next target."

"And how do we stop them?"

Dominic grinned. "Simple. We find them first."

Chapter 16

Harrington had spread a map across the hood of her SUV, the location of the burning hulk of the former data center circled in red.

"Here's what we know," she said. "There were fifteen guys manning this outpost. Five technicians who took care of the mainframes, and ten security personnel. Highly armed, highly trained. Not the kind of guys you screw with unless you know what you're doing."

"And did they?" Dominic stood with his arms akimbo, staring down at the map.

"Well, there's a reason there are so many bodies at the site. We counted fifty. I don't know how well-trained they were. But they were certainly committed."

"So, a massed force hits the site head on. Overwhelms security, makes their way down to the lower level, blows the place to hell."

"That's about right. It will be a while before we can get a team down to the core, but I think we can assume they had some inside knowledge, too. They knew where to hit, and they knew how to take the place down."

"Where do we go from here?"

Harrington picked up her DNA scanner and began tapping on the screen.

"We've identified fifty-five distinct DNA signatures in the wreckage. Our techs are separating out the signatures of our suspects from the deceased now. We're here," Harrington said, pointing at the circle. "Everything south of the center is inhabited. It's possible they'd go south, try and blend in. But something tells me they wouldn't do that. Something tells me they'd run north, try and hide among the ruins of north DC. That's what I'd do at least."

Marcus glanced at Dominic, and he could see the gears turning.

"I trust your judgment," Dominic said. "And I think you're probably right. We divide the north between us. If they did go north, it helps us. Nobody much goes up there anymore, so look for signs of life. Use your scanners, and shoot first, ask questions later. These guys are as dangerous as they come. They'll be armed, and they don't care who they kill. Especially if it's one of us."

* * *

Five minutes later, Marcus and Dominic were headed north, the column of smoke disappearing in the rearview mirror. Marcus had his rifle sitting in his lap. Dominic had insisted that he have it loaded and ready to go. He'd had him strap on a Spiker as well. What they'd face, he didn't know, but Dominic expected a quick and dirty operation, one where they might have to strike hard, strike fast, and move on.

"Were you in Asia for the whole war?"

"Yeah," Marcus said. The war had been on his mind, and he guessed it had been on Dominic's as well. "First with the Australians in Indonesia. And then, when that bogged down, I was transferred to the First Expeditionary. I was with them when we took Vladivostok, and then all the way to Luoyang."

"Vladivostok. What was that like?"

Marcus chuckled. "You've heard, I'm sure."

"Hell man, hearing ain't seeing."

Marcus looked down at his hands. They didn't shake anymore. Not like they used to. "No, no I guess it's not. Vladivostok was cold. That's what I remember the most. It was so cold. And people made mistakes because of it. The Ashkhani had cleared out the city. Bombs were everywhere. Even on the bodies.

And the buildings, damn. They were experts at demolition. One time, I remember watching this high-rise apartment building come down on top of an entire division. They didn't have a chance. Buried alive. And we didn't have the equipment or the time to try and get them out. I don't know how many made it, if any. What about you? Where were you?"

"Europe."

"Gibraltar?"

"Calais."

Calais. Marcus shuddered. If the seas had ever run red with blood, it was at Calais. The invasion had failed, the beachhead shattered. Thousands—tens of thousands—had died. Many more were taken prisoner. They were summarily executed, as was the way of the Ashkhani.

"How did you make it out?"

Dominic shrugged. "Dumb, stupid luck. My unit was pinned down on the northern part of the invasion zone, along the docks. We were fortunate. There were places to hide. Still, most of my guys surrendered. Maybe I would have too if I hadn't gotten separated. I hid out in an abandoned warehouse, dodging Ashkhani patrols. Killed a lot of men on my way out of the city. By the time I got to the countryside, I was hungry, dehydrated, pretty much on the verge of collapse. A man found me out there, a farmer, and took me back to his place. He and his family nursed me back to health. It was just lucky they found me. If it had been anybody else, I probably wouldn't be here. Anyway, once I was back on my feet I headed south to hook up with the force coming up from Gibraltar. Made it for the fall of Paris."

"Did you ever see the family again?"

Dominic nodded. "Yeah. I went back, when the war ended. Wanted to thank them. But I guess somebody knew what they'd done. Or maybe somebody just decided they weren't loyal enough to the Khan. Either way, I found the farmer, his wife, and his two kids in the farmhouse. They'd been gutted. I burned the place down around them. Seemed the only thing to do."

Some part of Marcus wanted to be shocked by this story, but he'd heard so many like it before. He'd even told a few himself.

"The world gone mad," Marcus said.

"You asked me yesterday how I do this job. I can do it because I believe the world did go mad, and it could go mad again. We are the only thing keeping it sane."

The car radio came alive with a screech. Dominic picked up the receiver. "This is Miles."

"Call just came in to central dispatch over at the DC PD. An alarm was triggered at an abandoned building up on Alaska Avenue, near 12th. The guy who owns the place is apparently holding out hope that real estate is due for a recovery."

"We'll head up there and check it out. Did you wave off the PD?"

"Yeah, we took care of it. It's all yours. Need backup?"

Dominic looked at Marcus and winked. "I think we can take this one on our own."

Dominic hit the gas, the roar of the engine the only sound for miles.

Chapter 17

A block from the building, Dominic stopped the car.

"Let's go on foot. No reason to let 'em know we're coming."

The city was silent, in only the way a silent city can be. So when Dominic slammed a clip into his rifle and chambered a round, it sounded to Marcus like thunder.

"So much for stealthy huh?"

Dominic ignored him. "Just remember. Shoot first. Ask questions later. If we can take them alive, great. We need the intel. But I don't want to lose any more guys today, either. You got me?"

"I got you."

The two men moved down the road, the early afternoon sun beating down upon them. They made no effort to hide themselves, and Marcus felt horribly exposed. Abandoned buildings loomed on every side, and Marcus could imagine the eyes of shooters peering down on him from any number of shattered windows.

Dominic didn't seem concerned. He crouched low, advancing quickly but steadily, his eyes fixed downrange. He swung his gun back and forth, scanning the horizon, looking for targets. Marcus hung behind him, ready to provide covering fire if it was needed. When they came to the end of the block, Dominic held up a hand, signaling Marcus to stop.

"Door's cracked," he whispered. "Somebody's inside. Could be our target. Could be a vagrant, but that's doubtful. Plenty of better places closer to the city center for squatters. Let's go, but stay tight. Could also be a trap."

"Should we really walk into it then?"

Dominic shrugged. "Nobody to call for backup. Our crews are spread all over the city, and somebody's got to go. If it's your day, it's your day, right? Besides, what you got to live for?"

Dominic jogged toward the complex, with Marcus following close behind. The two men never took their eyes from their gun sights, though Marcus figured if anyone was waiting, they'd take a shot before Dominic and Marcus even saw them. But his worst thoughts were for naught, as they reached the shelter of the doorway without incident.

Dominic pointed at himself, then jerked a thumb toward the door. Marcus nodded and tightened his grip on his rifle. Dominic reached out and eased the door open, letting it swing wide in a long, slow arc, a high-pitched creak ringing through the empty hallway. He ducked his head inside just long enough to see, but hopefully not so long that he'd catch a bullet, then looked at Marcus and nodded toward the door. Then he swung his weapon around and went inside.

Marcus followed, the two men hugging the wall. The hallway ended in another door, one that led to an open floor space. It was an old office building, and a sea of cubicles waited ahead of them. The look on Dominic's face said it all—this was not a good development. Whoever they were looking for could be hiding in any of them, waiting to take their shot.

The power in the building was off, the only light filtering in through large windows that lined the side of the far wall. It was a death trap, and Marcus waited while Dominic stared out over the long-abandoned desks.

He finally tapped Marcus on the chest and pointed at a doorway perpendicular to where they stood. Getting to it would mean hugging the outer wall of the room with the cubicles, but at least they wouldn't have to go in amongst them. There was the danger that the door would be locked, or that it would only lead to a closet or a storage area, but what other choice did they have?

As they crept along the wall in the fading light and cascading dust, Marcus marveled at just how exposed they still were. It was only then he realized how important the chase was for Dominic. For all his promises of caution, for all his protests that they stay safe, he simply wanted his quarry and would do whatever it took to get it.

Fears about the door were misplaced. It opened on the lightest touch, swinging wide to reveal a darkened hallway that led to more offices. Dominic stepped forward but then jerked to a stop. He threw up a hand, craning his neck so that one ear pointed down the length of the hallway. Marcus raised his rifle and stood stone-still. The two men remained in that position for a full minute. Marcus was tempted to ask what they were doing.

But then he heard it.

A voice trickling out of one of the far offices. A whisper that often broke into sound, one pleading for help. But not just help, *extraction*. It was that word, that very *military* term, that told them what they needed to know.

Marcus felt those first changes that the body experiences when the fight-or-flight mechanism kicks in. The increased heart rate, the fast, shallow breathing. The narrowing of the vision and palms filled with sweat. A thousand scenarios ran through his mind. Armed terrorists ready to kill. A gun fight that might end his life. Murder and death seemed a given, and Marcus remembered all that he had learned in the war, back when he never assumed he would make it home. When life could end as suddenly as it had begun.

Dominic advanced down the hallway, quickly, but light on his feet. He made not a sound, and Marcus tried to keep up. They reached the doorway, and it was obvious that whoever was inside didn't hear them; their requests for help continued. Dominic glanced at Marcus and raised his eyebrows. Marcus nodded.

The two men burst into the room. Marcus expected shouted commands, chaos, gunshots maybe. Instead, silence. That is, until Dominic started to laugh.

"Well, well, well," he said. "What do we have here?"

Chapter 18

She was dressed in black. Black shirt tucked into black pants. Her hair was pulled back behind her head, tied in a ponytail. She was sixteen, seventeen at the oldest. She was clutching a phone in her hand, but her eyes were on Marcus and Dominic.

Dominic chuckled. Marcus's eyes darted from him to her, wondering what it meant. The look of shock on the girl's face was soon replaced by understanding as she studied the men in front of her. Heavily armed, no visible identification, Spikers hanging from their belts. Marcus could see she was no longer filled with confusion or fear, but with pure malice.

"Shepherds," she whispered.

"Ah yes," Dominic said, "so we understand each other. How refreshing."

The girl flipped her phone closed and started to put it back in her pocket. Dominic gestured with the business end of his rifle.

"Nuh uh uh, little lady. Why don't you keep those hands where I can see them."

"I don't know who you think you are," she said, raising her hands above her head. "But you can't keep me here."

"Oh I think we can, and I think you know exactly why we're here. You see this?" Dominic pointed at the portable DNA sniffer attached to his belt. "This little baby is going to tell me everything I'd ever want to know about you. Who you are, where you're from, when you were born, where you go to school, your parents' names, your boyfriend's name. It might even tell me what you had for breakfast. And if I was a betting man, I'd say it will also match the DNA we took from a little fire down the road that you might know something about. What do you say to that?"

The girl glared at him. "I guess you'll do what you have to do."

Dominic chuckled again. He lowered his rifle and said, "You do anything stupid and my friend here is going to shoot you. You understand?" She didn't answer. Dominic shook his head and pulled the scanner free. "I've been dealing with you people for almost twenty years, and you're all the same." He turned to Marcus. "She looks all young and innocent, doesn't she? But she's a killer on the inside. Isn't that right?"

Dominic tapped his passcode into the scanner and pointed it at the girl. "I always wonder, why do you do what you do? Was it something your parents did? Or is it something. . ."

Dominic trailed off, and Marcus only barely heard him mumble, ". . . in the genes," before he went silent.

Marcus had been afraid before. He'd been terrified of death, many times. But he'd never felt as unsettled, as disturbed, as he did the moment he saw Dominic's face. The color drained away. His mouth went slack. Marcus even thought he was trembling. The supreme confidence was gone, the sense of ultimate control, vanished. Dominic was staring at the girl with an almost overwhelming expression of fear.

She smiled.

The DNA scanner fell to the ground, its display shattering. Dominic reached down and pulled the rifle to his shoulder, and Marcus could read in his eyes what he intended to do—he was going to kill her.

"You . . ." Dominic mumbled.

"Woah, woah, woah," Marcus said, throwing up his hands. "Dominic, what the hell are you doing?"

Still, the girl smiled. "Are you going to shoot me, officer? Is that what you intend? What happened to your law, your order?"

"The law says you die," Dominic growled.

The three of them stood alone in the abandoned building, in that silent tomb, and yet Marcus could barely hear over the pounding of blood in his own skull. "Dominic, put the gun down, man."

"She's Reborn, Ryder! This is what we do."

"What are you talking about! She's only a kid."

"Yeah, well what do you think happens when we don't get them early on?"

Marcus didn't have time to think. He raised his rifle and pointed it at Dominic's temple. Dominic never took his gun off the girl. He turned his head to look at Marcus as if the will that it took to do so was almost more than he could manage. In his eyes was a cold fury.

"I thought I told you never to point a gun at me again."

"I can't let you do this. I can't let you murder her in cold blood. Let's just take her in. Let's just take her in and let the cops handle it."

Dominic started to laugh, but there was no humor there. It was a laugh filled with pity. Pity for a fool.

"The cops? You want to call the cops? No, Marcus. We don't get to pull that card. There's nobody but us and them. Us, and her. This is what you signed up for. You shoot me and you might as well put a bullet in your own head. And if you let *her* go, you might as well put a bullet in the head of everyone you ever loved."

The gun trembled in Marcus's hand. He couldn't count how many men he'd killed, and he didn't want to know. But he couldn't shoot Dominic. And Dominic knew it.

Dominic turned back to the girl, who hadn't moved. If she was afraid, she didn't show it. If Dominic expected her to beg for her life, she wasn't about to give him the pleasure.

"I don't know how you lived this long," he said. "I don't know how you got away from us before you were born. But I thank the God that watches over us that you did. You believe in fate, right? That's what you taught, wasn't it? That's what you told the ones who followed you? That everything happens for a reason? That it was ordained to be? To fulfill some great plan? Well I believe in fate, too. And I believe fate brought you to this place for a reason. So that I could be the one to put a bullet in your skull. So I could be the one to kill you."

Dominic steadied his rifle. His finger tightened around the trigger. The girl held her hands out to her side and closed her eyes.

There was a whine, a high-pitched tone. A flash of blue light filled the room. For a moment Dominic stood there, eyes on the girl, finger on the trigger. But then he collapsed into a heap. The Spiker felt so heavy in Marcus's hand that he dropped it to the ground, where it landed with a hollow clatter.

"Oh God," he said. "What have I done?"

Chapter 19

He stood over Dominic's motionless body, and for an instant he thought he might be dead. But then the man let out a low moan and began to stir. The girl didn't wait. Before Marcus could react, she bolted for the door.

"Stop!"

Marcus reached out to grab her but caught only air. He hesitated, looking back at Dominic. But it was no use. He couldn't believe what he'd done, but now was no time for regrets. He went after the girl, leaving his old partner behind.

She spun down the hallway, racing into the large room filled with cubicles. Marcus followed, now heedless of the danger. He was going on instinct, and he knew she was alone. He expected her to cut toward the front door, but at the last moment she turned left. Marcus stumbled over his own legs and went spiraling to the ground, crashing into a cubicle wall which promptly gave way and landed on his prone body. He pushed it off and pulled himself to his feet. By the time he'd resumed the chase, he'd lost sight of her.

Fortunately, there was only one other way to go, and he saw her again as she opened the rear emergency exit and burst out into the dying light of the afternoon. He followed, throwing wide the door and rushing out into the empty lot behind the building.

He stopped for a moment, scanning the area, looking for his quarry. He saw her scaling a fence at the far end and sprinted across the vacant field of dead grass, broken concrete, and smashed beer bottles. He reached the chain-link perimeter just as she was going over.

She landed on the other side, dropping on all fours like a cat.

"Wait!"

For a few precious seconds, she froze. They stood there, staring at one another across the tiny gulf, separated only by thin metal wires. He looked in her pale blue eyes and saw a combination of fear and excitement, the energy of the chase, the thrill of being pursued.

He held out his hand, palm forward. "Please. Just wait."

But the magic was broken by the wail of police sirens in the distance. He turned to look in the direction of the sound, and when he turned back she was running. As much as he hated to admit it, as much as it shocked him, he realized that those sirens were as much for him as they were for her.

He began to climb. He landed with a thud on the other side, nowhere near as gracefully, a sharp pain shooting through his knees as he struck the pavement. He stumbled off down the alley just as she turned a corner. By the time he reached it, she had wrenched up a manhole cover and was sliding it, with not inconsiderable difficulty, to the side. Without a second look, she dropped away into nothingness.

Marcus didn't hesitate. He ran to the hole in the earth and, putting one foot below the other, began to clamber down the wrought-iron ladder that descended into the black void waiting below. Solid ground did not await him at the bottom. Instead, his feet splashed into a fetid pool of dank water. The absence of light was nearly complete, and he began to panic as he realized the only illumination came from above.

The panic didn't last long, and by the time he heard the sound in the night, it was too late. The sharp pain in the back of his head lasted only a second before he passed into the even greater darkness of unconsciousness.

* * *

When Dominic came to, he flipped over onto his belly and vomited. The contents of his stomach landed with one great splat at the feet of Harrington. He tried to steady himself, but his efforts to rise brought another wave of nausea. He fell to his knees again, gagging and dry heaving, the world spinning uncontrollably.

"You've looked better," Harrington said.

Dominic hugged the ground like a man on a ship in a storm, and despite his best efforts he could not set the world back on its axis.

"What's wrong with me?" he managed.

"It will pass. Just give it time. Someone hit you with a Spiker. But damned if I know anything more than that. What's going on, Dominic? When you didn't report back, we tracked your vehicle to this area. Found it about a block down from here. Searched all the buildings in the neighborhood till we found you. What the hell happened?"

"Marcus. Marcus has gone rogue."

"Good God," Harrington said. "This day just keeps getting better."

Dominic wiped the spittle from his face and managed to meet her eyes.

"Just wait. It's about to get a whole lot worse."

Chapter 20

Marcus knew he was dreaming. He'd had this dream before. He still felt the concussion from every shell, still heard the bullets whizzing past his ear, still smelled the blood and felt the fear.

They'd rained down shells on Luoyang for four days, battering the city like the storm that continued to rage throughout the bombardment. The generals theorized that by the time they had finished, the army could march into the city and take it with barely a shot fired. But the theory had proved wanting.

When the artillery fell silent, the shouts of the Ashkhani rose up from the rubble, echoing across the hills. Now every pile of debris became a strongpoint, every collapsed building a redoubt, every shell crater a bunker.

Marcus and Halo Company picked their way down the hillside into the maze of burning wreckage and waiting death below. Their orders were simple—take the city, neutralize any opposition, capture Khan if found. That last order was very specific. Capture, not kill. They wanted Khan alive.

But it was all folly. Luoyang was chaos and blood. Half of Halo Company was dead before they'd cleared the perimeter road that surrounded the city. Formations were broken. Order was lost. It was every man for himself.

In the dream, Marcus was running down an alley. Bullets peppered the walls. Shells exploded around him. Dust coated his face and choked his lungs. There was a sudden feeling like he'd been punched in the shoulder and he found himself tumbling along the ground through a broken doorway in the concrete shell of an old building.

His hand went to his shoulder and came away covered in blood. He looked down at it and started to laugh. He'd made it so far, through so many fights, so many battles, always expecting to die. And yet he'd never been wounded, never even touched. But it seemed his luck had run out. At least he was still alive. That was worth something.

He picked himself up, using the butt of his gun as a crutch. He was so tired, so sore. Every part of him ached. He checked his rifle. Everything was intact. He'd need it. He was cut off from his unit, what was left of it. He felt the wound on his arm. The bleeding had lessened, but he was still injured and alone.

He glanced around the crumbling structure, and considered that perhaps he could hide out until the battle was over. As best he could tell, it was some sort of government building. A great flag still hung from the rafters, the standard of the Khan, a purple banner with a falcon—wings spread wide as if one were looking down on it in midflight—in the center. It was while he looked upon that hated banner, the one beneath which so many had died, that he saw something he did not expect.

There was a bank of cables that ran from the ceiling, down along the wall to the floor. They originally disappeared behind what looked to be a solid, concrete slab. The violence of the bombardment had shoved the slab to the side, revealing a corridor.

Marcus slung the strap of his rifle around his good shoulder and walked to the opening. The corridor was actually a stairway leading down. The cables followed along the ceiling into the depths of whatever was below. Machine-gun fire echoed through the alleyway. He didn't stop to think. He stepped into the opening and descended.

His eyes adjusted to the gloom, the pale bulbs that illuminated the stairwell providing just enough light to see. Marcus led with his rifle. He fully expected to stumble upon a battalion of Ashkhani warriors at any moment. Yet the place seemed utterly deserted. As the stairway leveled out, he found barracks and dining halls and even recreation areas, but no people. Whoever had been here before had left in haste. Probably to defend the city.

Marcus crept down the hallway, careful not to make a sound. There was a door at the end of the corridor. It was the only door he had seen so far that had been closed. He gripped tight his rifle and advanced. He wasn't sure how he knew it, but some preternatural sense told him that this room was not empty. He had another feeling, too, one he couldn't so easily describe. He'd felt it every night in his dreams, the decades after that fateful day, and yet what precisely it meant eluded him. He gripped the handle of the door, said a silent prayer that he hoped someone heard, and pulled.

It revealed what must have been a command center. Maps lined the wall, both physical ones and digital projections. There was a bank of computers on one side, next to communications equipment. A long wooden table sat in the middle. At the far end of that table sat a man, one who Marcus had only seen before in pictures.

Many nights he had had the dream, and every time it was the same. Marcus lived it, but he was a slave to it as well, for he could not change it. He was doomed, under the whip of that old master, time, like a specter in a castle who forever relives the night of his execution. Every night he did the same thing he did on that day years before, the last day of the war.

He saw Khan standing at the end of the table, and Khan saw him. The two locked eyes. Khan held out his arms to his sides, palms forward. He closed his eyes and tilted back his head. And Marcus Ryder shot him three times in the heart. That is what Marcus had seen so many nights in his dreams—the moment that he murdered Khan.

What made it so unusual this night was that something had changed.

Khan stood at the end of the table as they locked eyes. Then something unexpected. Khan smiled. Not a haughty smile or a mocking smile, but one filled with pity, with understanding. Even as Marcus stood there with his rifle aimed at the man's heart, he felt completely disarmed.

"We meet again, Marcus Ryder. How far you have come. How much you have suffered. All your life, you searched for meaning, for purpose. To be remembered. To accomplish something of consequence. Yet look at you now."

Marcus watched, and listened. Even though he heard him, Khan's mouth never moved. Nor was the voice what he had expected, the voice he had heard so many times on recordings and broadcasts. This was different.

"How many times I would have gathered you in my arms like a father gathers up his children. But you refused me. You rejected me.

Content in your own wisdom. Sure in your own path. You, like sheep, have gone astray. You are the prodigal, and I am the all-father. The time of your choosing is at hand.

"Choose wisely."

Marcus felt the strength leave him, and he collapsed to the ground, the vast shadow falling over him.

* * *

A helicopter flew overhead and cast a powerful beam of light on the empty lot where Dominic stood, hands in his pockets. He had two dozen men searching the area for Marcus. He couldn't have gone far alone and on foot, but Dominic had a feeling they wouldn't find him. The girl was the wildcard. He'd gone after her, and if he wasn't dead, then he was probably with her. Dominic saw Harrington walking across the field toward him. She had her phone out.

"Just got a call from Butterfield's sweeper team." She pointed to the fence at the end of the lot. "They found an unknown DNA sequence at the top of the fence."

"Is it a match for the one we found at the data center?"

Harrington shook her head. "They can't say. It's pretty degraded. Butterfield says it's a fifty-fifty shot. He says it's mixed in with some kind of substance he can't identify."

Dominic figured as much. They were using something to mask the DNA signature. It was the only thing that made sense. Otherwise, the girl would have set off alarms all over the city every time she went outside.

"One thing he's sure of, though, is that Marcus went over that fence. He got a 100% match from a patch of soil on the other side."

Dominic shook his head and spat on the ground. Marcus did go with her. He wasn't surprised. Just disappointed.

"Dominic," Harrington said softly, her tone turning personal, "what the hell happened back there? They tried to get a reading off of your DNA scanner but it was smashed."

Dominic grinned. That was his fault. "Yeah, I guess I dropped it."

Harrington just stared at him. "You dropped it? That's it?"

Dominic wanted to tell her. He wanted to tell her everything he knew, everything that had been shared with him years before, when he had been one of the first members of the Shepherds. He knew he could trust her. They'd been close before, once. What seemed like a very long time ago. But some secrets had to be kept.

"You know, during the war," he said, "it was revenge that kept me going. Pure hate, you know? I wanted to kill every Ashkhani son of a bitch I could get my hands on. For what they'd done. For what they wanted to do."

Harrington walked over and sat on the bumper of the SUV parked at the edge of the field, where Dominic was standing. She clasped her hands between her legs, looking up at him. "I try not to think about them," she said. "It's like a nightmare, what happened then. Something we'll tell our kids about but they won't believe. They're still hunting down Ashkhani all over Europe, you know. Half of Africa's still under their control. Sometimes I wonder if we will ever be rid of them."

"What if they come back?" Dominic said.

"The Ashkhani? No, Dom. That's different and you know it. People weren't born Ashkhani. They became them. They were a disease, a cult. No, people might be born murderers. But it takes something especially evil to create something like the Ashkhani. It takes someone like Khan."

"And what about him? Could he come back?" Dominic said. "He's always been with us, in one form or fashion. There's always someone who thinks he should rule the world. Maybe it's just always been him."

Harrington shuddered. "God, I hope not. I don't think we could take that, not after everything that's happened."

He needed a drink, and he needed one badly. Instead he walked over and put his arm around Harrington. "But that's why we are here, right? To keep something like that from ever happening? To protect people? To protect the sheep from the wolves?"

Harrington nodded. "That's why I'm here. I never saw combat in the war. I was too young. Joined as soon as I could though. My father insisted. But by the time I got to the front it was over. I felt cheated, you know? Like I had let everyone down. And I knew that the war would always be everything there was, for all my life. There would be those who fought and those who didn't. And the ones who didn't would live in shame, till the end. So when I got a chance to do this, I took it."

Dominic shook his head and laughed. "It's funny you put it that way. I'd never wish what I saw on anybody. Not a soul. And if they got out of it, then better for them."

"Sometimes I think we are still at war," Harrington said.

Dominic removed a cigarette from his pocket and lit it. He inhaled deeply and blew a column of smoke into the darkening sky. "And we always will be. And now Marcus is in the belly of the beast with the enemy."

"I don't even understand," Harrington said. "Who are these people, and why would they do this?"

Dominic shrugged his shoulders, as if he didn't know the answer. But he did. He just couldn't say. And he doubted she could take it if he did.

Harrington shook her head. "We don't even know where to start looking."

"We don't," Dominic said. "Not yet. But I have a pretty good idea who does."

Chapter 21

He floated through the darkness, and words he could not place surrounded him, a name that seemed familiar.

"He's coming to, Faðirin."

When Marcus awoke, he couldn't move anything but his head. For one horrible instant, he thought something had happened that he had forgotten, that perhaps he was paralyzed. But then his muscles flexed against the bonds that held him and he realized the situation was much more dire. He was being held captive, by whom he couldn't say. He looked around the room, but he hadn't gotten far when he saw her.

She was sitting in a chair in a ratty white t-shirt and jeans without shoes or socks. She had her knees pulled tight against her chest, and all he could see of her face were her eyes. In that moment, he couldn't help but think how young she looked.

"You're awake," she said. She waited for Marcus to say something, and when he didn't, she added, "I'm sorry about the restraints. I'm sure you understand."

Marcus jerked his arm up against the straps and the girl jumped in her seat. They held.

"Please don't do that," she said. "There's really no point."

"I can see that," he said. Marcus knew how this was going to go. It was obvious why they hadn't killed him. Yet, at least. He had information, information they wanted. They'd torture him until they had it and then they would kill him. It wouldn't be quick; he'd pay for his compassion. Or whatever it was that had caused him to pull his Spiker and fire it at Dominic's head.

"I wanted to thank you."

He wouldn't have thought it possible, but he started to laugh. "You wanted to thank me?"

"Yeah, for saving my life." She seemed genuinely confused.

"Saving your life?"

"That's what you did, isn't it? You could have let him shoot me, but you stopped him."

Marcus fell silent, and so did the girl. She stared at him, her bright green eyes shining in the dim light that streamed in from thin windows set high in the wall.

"So," she said stretching her legs out in front of her, "what's your name?"

"Marcus," he said. "Marcus Ryder. I'm a police officer. You can't keep me here."

"I don't make those decisions. You'll have to talk to Colonel Thiessen about that."

Marcus frowned. "Right. I'll get on that." He looked around at the barren walls and saw nothing that could help him. "So," he said, "what should I call you?"

"Alex," she said. "Alexandra Dunn."

"And how old are you, Alexandra Dunn."

"Sixteen," she said. "But I'll be seventeen in August…"

She didn't finish, instead letting the unspoken "if I live" hang in the air. He simply nodded in response.

"What did your machine tell you about me?"

"I think you know," Marcus said.

She smiled. "You can't imagine what it's like. People say that all the time I guess, and usually it's not true. But when I was born, even before I was born, somebody, somewhere, had already decided that I had to die. Weighed, measured, and found wanting. Can you believe that? Have you ever thought about it that way, Marcus? When you were hunting people down and killing them. You said you're a cop, right, but that's not exactly true. You see," she said, leaning forward and pointing a finger at him, "you think you know about me because you ran a DNA test or whatever. But I know about you, too. I know what you've done."

"What I've done? Maybe you should look in the mirror. I've seen your handiwork. I was at the facility you destroyed today. Sixteen years old. Sitting over there like you are a child. Like you're an innocent. How many men have you killed? Huh? No, I know who *you* are because of what *you've* done. It seems to me that you're living up to your legacy just fine."

She started to laugh, but she choked it off and shook her head. "Do you think I wanted to kill those men? Do you think I want any part of this? Do you think, if I had a choice, that my entire life wouldn't be different? I do what I have to do, Marcus. You know that. You were a soldier."

Marcus nodded his head.

"My mother used to tell me a story, before she was killed by men like you. A long time ago, there were two boys who were born in two very different places. They both loved to read. They both loved to hike and to camp. But when they were only a little bit older than me, their two countries went to war, and both the boys were sent off to fight. It was the night before a big battle when one of the boys wandered off into the woods with a bottle of whiskey he'd stolen from an officer's tent. He knew he'd probably die the next day, so he figured he might as well enjoy the night. When he came to a river, the boy stumbled upon the other young man, sitting on a rock and smoking a pipe. The two pulled their guns and pointed them at each other. But then the one boy saw the other's whiskey, while the other admired the pipe. 'A trade?' one of them asked. The other nodded, and for the next two hours they sat on the rock together, smoking their pipe and drinking their whiskey, as friends. But the night could not last forever, and as the moon began to set, the two boys rose and shook hands. 'Good luck to you, Johnny Reb,' the one said. 'Good luck to you, Billy Yank,' the other one answered. And the next day, they took up arms. The next day, the two boys who had parted as friends tried to kill each other. Now let me ask you this, Marcus—do you think either one of those boys *wanted* to kill the other? Do you think if they had the chance to leave that place, to live together in peace and friendship, they wouldn't have seized that opportunity without a thought?

"I don't want to fight, Marcus. But I'll die if I don't. I'll probably never live to see my twentieth birthday. And all because of something completely out of my control. So you go ahead and assume you can tell me what my legacy is or should be. I'm just trying to survive. It's a miracle I've made it this far."

The door opened, and in walked a woman much older than Alexandra. Her face was stern, her straw-colored hair pulled tight in a ponytail that hung over the back of a utilitarian black shirt tucked into khaki pants. Marcus always knew when he was in the presence of a veteran of the war. This woman was one of them.

"Alex," she said, "can you give us a moment?"

The girl said nothing. She popped up from her chair, cast a glance back at Marcus, and then walked out the door. The woman reached over and closed it.

"I'd shake your hand, but you'll see I'm a little restrained."

She stood at the edge of the bed, her hands behind her back.

"I'm sorry about that, Captain. But it couldn't be helped."

"I see you've done your research."

She nodded once, quickly. "My name is Pamela Thiessen. I was a colonel in the war, under General Donnelly."

"Then you were at Luoyang."

Another curt nod. "You don't remember me, Captain, but it was my unit that found you that day, after Khan. I'm guessing you don't remember much of anything from then."

Marcus shuddered, and as much as he wanted to hide it, he knew Thiessen saw. When she looked away and out the high window, it only confirmed it. It was true, of course. He didn't remember anything of that day. Something inside of him had broken in Luoyang. His last real memory was going into the city. The next thing he knew he was in a hospital. Everything in between had only come back in his dreams months later. And he often wondered if he only dreamed of killing Khan because others had told him about it.

"But why are you here? Why are you helping her?"

Thiessen turned and glanced at the door. "That girl?" she said, pointing. "Because she is an innocent. And I think the innocent should be defended."

"Innocent? How can you say that?"

"You tell me. If she was so guilty, if she was who you think she is, then why didn't you kill her?"

Marcus fell silent. It was a question he could not answer. Whatever she was supposed to be, in that moment, with Dominic's gun pointed at her head and his finger on the trigger, she had only been a scared girl.

"That's a question you'll have to answer for yourself, eventually, when you decide who you are and who you are fighting for. We protect her because she is a child, because she doesn't deserve to die. She helps us here, and we don't normally let her out. But today we needed her, and it was worth the risk."

"You destroyed the data center."

Thiessen nodded. "We did."

"Why?"

"I'll be completely honest with you, Captain. Your presence here is an unexpected complication. We can't let you go, as I'm sure you're well aware. You're a prisoner of an undeclared war. And so the question becomes what to do with you. It is my intention to keep you here. Against your will, yes. But unharmed. Until such time as I figure out somewhere else to put you. I can tell you, not everyone in the organization agrees with that decision. There are many here who, not unwisely, see you as a liability, a threat. If you were to escape, I am sure you would lead the men you work for back to this place and they would kill us all. Everything we have been working toward would be undone."

"And what exactly are you working toward?"

Thiessen smiled. "An end to madness. A madness that has gripped our country and the world since the end of the war. A madness where people are judged, placed in the balance and found wanting before they are even born."

"So you don't believe then? You're a denier?"

The colonel started to answer, but the words fell away. She grinned a half-smile, pulling a chair away from the wall. She fell as much as sat down into it, her whole body seeming to collapse. She drew in a deep breath and let it all out at once.

"I don't know what I believe, Captain Ryder. It's all . . . when this first started, it seemed like there was so much debate, controversy. And then the war came. And after the war, everyone just wanted peace. Security. They wanted things to go back to the way they were. And somehow the only way to do that was to change everything. So all that we fought for, our freedom, our humanity, it just seemed like it was gone. But I know that girl, Captain. I know the girl whose life you saved, even though you knew what she was supposed to be. I found her myself, when she was eight years old, wandering the streets on the edge of the city. She was digging around in a trashcan looking for food. Her parents were dead, killed sometime earlier. I never found out exactly when. It's not something she talks about. Truth is, it was a miracle, Captain, that she was even alive. It was a miracle that they had not found her. I took her in, and she's been with us ever since. We raised her, and we protected her. We've given her the things that every child should have. Love, friendship, education. A hope for the future. But she'll never be like every other child. And it has nothing to do with her genes. It's not about her status, whether she's Marked or Reborn or Clear. It's because she's grown up in a world where stepping outside these walls meant a chance that she'd run into somebody who was charged with killing her. Somebody like you. That's what I know, Captain. That's what I believe. But it's not all I know. And some of the things I know, you should know too."

She reached down and unclipped an old-fashioned walkie-talkie from her belt. "This is Colonel Thiessen, come back." There was a crackling on the other end in answer. "Send Jacob in."

A moment later, the door to Marcus's room opened. In walked a scrawny man who, from his torn jeans to his t-shirt to his wire-rimmed glasses, would not easily be mistaken for a revolutionary.

"This is Jacob Sievers."

"Can't say it's a pleasure to meet you," the man said. Marcus didn't laugh.

"Have a seat, Jake. Jacob is a recent addition to our group. Two months ago, he was not all that different from you."

"I was a records tech," he said. "With the Shepherds. The data center that was destroyed today? That was my duty station."

"So that's how you knew how to hit it," Marcus said, straining against his bonds. "That's how you knew how to get in. Because you sold them out. My God, man. How many of your friends died today because of what you did?"

Jacob didn't bother trying to meet Marcus's eyes. Instead he looked away and muttered, "It wasn't an easy decision."

"Before you judge him," said Thiessen, "hear him out."

Jacob stared down at his feet and began to speak. "About a year ago, my wife, Amy, got pregnant. We went down to the hospital to have her tested, you know? Checked out. When we got the results back . . . well, our little girl had the gene. So she was going to be one of them. The doctors told us that it was the law; we had to get rid of her. So of course that is what we were going to do. But when I filled out the paperwork and turned it in, the doctor came back and said that there had been some kind of mistake. That when they'd sent the documentation in to the processing center, it had overridden the tests.

"My wife, of course, was overjoyed. She wanted nothing more than to keep our baby. But something wasn't right. I worked in the data center so, you know, the next day at work I went in to see the chief and explained what happened. He got up, closed the door behind him, and put his arm around me. He said, 'People who work for us don't have to worry about such things. Consider it a bonus.' Then he sent me on my way, and the last thing he said before I left was that I shouldn't mention it to anyone.

"So then I was more curious. But I'm a records tech, you know, so I had access to all the documents, all the files on the server. I started going through them. Checking, cross-referencing all the different tests that had been performed over the last, I don't know, six months. And I began to notice something. First it was the addresses. If you live in McLean, your tests don't come back with bad news. It was the folks on the outskirts of town who got those results. And then I stumbled upon the override files. And I noticed that people who worked for us, people who worked in the government, people who were important, famous, influential, well-connected, it was their names that were in those files. Their kids weren't in danger. That's when I began to wonder. And one day, I couldn't deny it anymore. Then I was convinced."

"Convinced of what?"

"That all of it was a lie. Just another way to keep everyone in line."

"You asked me, Marcus," Colonel Thiessen said as the two men fell silent, "what I believed. I don't know what happens after we die. I don't know if we have all lived before or if we will live again. And I don't know if that determines who we will be. But I will tell you what I do know. They don't care about those things. All they care about is power . . . and control. You asked us who we are, Captain?

"We are the rebellion, and we want you to join us."

Chapter 22

Dominic filled two five-gallon canisters of gasoline and put them in the back of his SUV. Then he drove to McLean. He arrived at the home of Dr. and Mrs. Davis well after the sun had set. He hopped out of the truck, whistling an old Johnny Cash song. He grabbed the two gas cans and walked up the drive. He barely broke stride when he reached the door, kicking it in with such force that it split the wood down the middle, jerking it off one of the hinges. A man cursed from somewhere in the depths of the house.

Doctor Davis ran into the foyer, his wife right behind him.

"What the hell is this?" he shouted, but the last word had barely left his lips when Dominic drew his gun and blew out his kneecap. The man made a sound like a kicked dog and collapsed to the ground. The woman's hands turned to claws, and her face twisted into a mask of rage. She took one step forward, but Dominic didn't wait for her to take another. He shot her in the gut, and then she was on the ground next to her husband.

Dominic recommenced whistling.

He unscrewed the top of the first canister of gasoline. He began to pour its contents around the house, splashing it on the drapes, cascading it down the bookshelf, dousing the flowers, soaking the furniture. He managed to cover the entire downstairs floor with the first can, tossing it away into the kitchen when he was finished. The second can had a special purpose.

He unscrewed the top and walked over to where the doctor and his wife were squirming in their own blood, kicking the man once in the knee for emphasis. He held the can high in the air, flipping it upside down so that the fuel poured like a waterfall down on the people at his feet. Their shrieks of pain when the caustic liquid hit their open wounds put a smile on Dominic's face.

When the can was empty, he shook it three times just to make sure he got every last drop, and then flung it across the living room, smashing a vase. He looked down at his clothes and was pleased to see he'd avoided dousing himself in the process.

He grabbed the only chair that wasn't covered in gasoline and pulled it in front of the two sobbing people. He spun it around backwards, straddling it as he sat down and rested his chin on the polished wood. And then for the first time since he'd arrived, he spoke.

"The last time I was here, there was a lot of bullshit. We're not doing any bullshit this time." Mrs. Davis had stopped screaming, and Dominic wondered if she'd screamed so much her vocal cords had been shredded.

"What do you want?" asked the doctor.

"Well here's the thing, doc, I let you off easy last time. I had my impressionable, young partner and all. But you weren't just hiding that girl. This wasn't a one-time thing for you. You're a part of something bigger. So I'm going to ask you some questions, and you are going to tell me the truth. The first time you lie to me, I'm going to blow out your other knee cap. It might set you on fire, it might not, who knows? Awful lot of gasoline. The second time you lie to me, I'm going to burn this place down around you. So the way I see it, you either tell me the truth, or you and your wife die screaming. You got me?"

The terror in the man's eyes confirmed that he did.

"So let's start with the easy one—you are part of this group, right?"

The doctor hesitated. Dominic slid his gun out of his holster. "Yes," he said, "yes."

"It's the same group that burned down a data center downtown today, right?"

"Yes, it is."

"And this group, they're the ones shipping these girls and their kids down South, right?"

"Yes."

"Excellent, doctor. This game is working out well for us so far. Now, you tell me where they're holed up. Where's their base of operations? Where do you get your orders?"

"I don't know," he said.

Dominic looked down at his 9 mm. He'd made a promise, and promises he normally kept. But he didn't mean to burn the man alive. Not yet, at least. He did, after all, need the information.

"Here's the thing," Dominic said, sliding the gun back in his holster and clapping his hands together. "I said no bullshit, so let's just cut to the chase." He reached inside his jacket pocket and removed a pack of cigarettes and a box of matches. He pulled one of the thin, white sticks from the package and let it dangle between his lips.

"This is what we're going to do," he said, the cigarette bouncing up and down with every word, "you tell me where they are, or I'm going to light this cigarette, and then I'm going to light you." He opened up the box and pulled a match from inside, holding it against the rough paper on the side. He looked at the doctor and raised his eyebrows.

"All right, all right, all right," the man said, holding up a hand, "all right, I'll tell you. The old red line, north of the city. The closed-off part. They took over one of the stations, Wheaton. That's how they get around. They use the underground. Sewers, subways, that kind of thing. Places you guys can't see them. Places the DNA scanners can't reach. You go there, you'll find them."

"Excellent," Dominic said. He stood up, flipping the chair around, sliding it back beneath the table. He started toward the door.

"But you won't win," the doctor said. "Not in the end. No matter how hard you try. No matter how many you kill. One day, you'll meet your fate. And then *he* will return."

Dominic stopped. He turned back and looked at the doctor over his shoulder, grinning, his cigarette still dangling from his lips. "We'll see about that."

He struck the match and touched it to the tip of the cigarette, drawing in a lungful of smoke. He breathed it out into the gathering dark. He flicked the tiny piece of burning wood behind him and was carried out into the coming night by the whoosh of igniting flames, the sound of desperate screams, and the smell of burning flesh.

Chapter 23

Alexandra was sitting in the chair watching him when Marcus woke up.

"Don't you ever sleep?"

"There's not a whole lot to do around here but sleep and train. So I have a lot of time on my hands. I'm sorry I didn't get to come back yesterday. I know we have a lot to talk about, and a lot to understand about each other."

Marcus sat up and rubbed the back of his neck. It took him a moment to realize he was no longer restrained.

"I talked to Colonel Thiessen about it," Alexandra said. "I didn't think you needed them anymore. Now that you know the truth. Was I wrong?"

"I appreciate that, but I'm still not sure I know what the truth is."

"All we ever know is what we see. In the past couple of days, you've seen a lot. Someone else, someone who hasn't gone through the things you've gone through, might not have made it out with their mind intact. In the end, I guess you have to find your own truth."

He swallowed a laugh. "Pretty wise for a sixteen-year-old. So, what's your truth then?"

Her green eyes flashed, and a shroud of sorrow seemed to fall over her. "My truth? That's a pretty interesting question. I won't lie to you. I've thought about it a lot. Plenty of time to think, and all. But I guess if I had to boil it down, I'd say this. I don't believe we live more than once, Marcus. Reincarnation, genetic rebirth, the soul—it doesn't matter what you call it. I don't believe in those things. I think this life is all we have. And that is a truly terrible thing."

"Some people might say that's comforting."

"They might, but they'd be lying. Maybe to you, maybe to themselves. It doesn't matter. All lies, nonetheless. People need hope, Marcus. We invent the next life—whether physical or spiritual, whether in Heaven or here upon the earth—to make the tragedies of this life more bearable."

"And you've seen your share?"

She nodded, and even that simple movement was pregnant with sorrow. "I have. And so have you."

He couldn't argue. Couldn't even start.

"So you've been here, all your life?"

"No," she said. "No, for a time I had a portion, albeit a small one, of normalcy. After Colonel Thiessen found me, she introduced me to a man and a woman. My new parents. He was a doctor, and she was a kind, childless lady who threw herself into me. They hid me when I needed hiding, but otherwise they treated me like I was their own."

"The Davises," Marcus whispered. She nodded.

"I wasn't the only one they saved. There's somebody else who wants to see you, Marcus."

She hopped up from her seat and opened the door.

The first thing Marcus saw was her eyes, the color of the sea after a storm. He gasped, pushing himself, almost involuntarily, back into the bed. But there was nowhere to run, nowhere to go to escape.

She'd been a girl when last he saw her only a couple of days before. Now she was a woman.

"I told them I wanted to kill you," she said. "But Colonel Thiessen talked me out of it. Not so tough without a gun, are you?"

"Rachel," Marcus tried to say, though his mouth, gone dry in the second she had entered, choked on the word. "I'm sorry."

She shook her head and crossed her arms, physically trying to hold herself together. "You had no right. No right. And you got no right to apologize to me now. How dare you? How dare you even think about it? You took something away and you can't give it back. You don't get any forgiveness. Not from me. Not from anyone. That's between you and God."

"But you knew that didn't you, Marcus?" The two of them turned to Alexandra, leaning against the far wall. "You regretted it from the moment you fired the shot. You never believed the lie. And yet that makes it worse, doesn't it? You knew her child was innocent, but you killed it anyway. For a job. For duty.

"That's why you saved me. Some hope for redemption you'll never receive. Some hope for forgiveness. But not from me, and not even from God. From Rachel. But she can't give you that, Marcus. You've taken all you can from her. If you are to redeem yourself, you'll have to do it another way."

"I . . . I don't know what to say."

Alexandra walked over to the open door and took hold of the handle. Rachel backed away, not taking her eyes off Marcus until she had passed out of the room. As Alexandra closed the door, she said, "Dr. and Mrs. Davis helped many people who were poor and desperate and hurting. But none loved them more than I did. I stayed with them until I was ready to help out here. Until I was ready to fight back." She turned and gazed at Marcus. "But I never forgot them. I never stopped loving them. Of all the sorrows I've seen, this is the worst—they were killed last night, Marcus. Burned to death in their own home."

"Oh my God. Dominic."

Alexandra nodded. "Yes. Your friend killed them to find you. And if I had to guess, I'd say he's on his way here, now."

An alarm sounded from somewhere far away. The door flew open and Thiessen entered, a rifle slung over her shoulder and two in her hands. "Looks like your boys found us. I guess it's time for you to make your choice." She handed one of the guns to Alexandra and threw the other to Marcus. He caught it in midair. "But whatever you decide, it needs to be now."

Marcus looked down at the rifle in his hand. He pulled back the slide and chambered a round. He clicked off the safety and looked at the two women standing before him.

"All right. Let's go."

Chapter 24

Dominic slid the tactical helmet over his head and felt the adrenaline pumping through his veins. It was the same rush that battle had always brought. He hadn't experienced it much since the war. Overnight, teams from surrounding states had converged on DC, and now Dominic and Harrington commanded more than a hundred heavily armed men and women. It would end here, today, Dominic thought. They were ready

"All right," he said. "We go in fast, and we go in hard. Shoot to kill. Don't take any unnecessary risks. If we break them here, well, we might just go a long way toward putting ourselves out of business."

Harrington was standing next to the bricked-up entrance that had once led down into the station below. One of the team's demolition experts was plugging detonators into blocks of C-4.

Harrington shook her head. "You sure you want to do this? It'd probably only take us ten minutes to break through this wall, and we could do it a lot quieter."

"I don't want it quiet. I want it loud. I want them to know we're coming."

"Well you're going to get your wish."

Dominic grinned. "What's the matter, Megs? Not up for a little fun?"

"I like it clean, Dom, you know that. Clean and easy."

"It will be, Megs. It will be. We're going to do something great today."

"I hope you're right."

"Oh, and Harrington, one other thing," Dominic said as he started to walk away. "Nobody touches Marcus. I want him for myself."

* * *

Marcus followed Alexandra and Thiessen out into a narrow hallway.

"Where are we?"

"The abandoned Wheaton stop. It's deep, allows us to move through the old subway and sewer systems. Your room was a storage area near the surface. We need to get down underground, and quickly."

The three of them reached a set of service stairs that descended to the tracks below. Thiessen led the way, running as fast as she could, dim lights that were strung from the ceiling providing the only illumination.

They were halfway down when an earthquake rumbled through the tunnels. Dust and loose stones poured from the ceiling, and Alexandra slipped. She pitched forward and would have gone tumbling down had Marcus not reached out and grabbed the back of her shirt. He pulled her tight against him, and the shaking girl looked back at him and smiled. "Thank you, Marcus. That's twice you've saved me."

"Explosion," Thiessen said. "They've broken through. Come on, we don't have much time."

They raced the rest of the way down the stairwell. Marcus couldn't shake the fear that at any moment bullets would rain down on them from above. When they reached the bottom, they met a picket line that had been set up to cover the evacuation. Two terrified boys were hunkered behind broken-down concrete barriers, their hands grasping shaking machine guns, inadequate, indeed, for whatever was coming. They faced a sloping stone ramp that led up to the main tunnels above.

"Colonel!" A man Marcus didn't recognize in tactical gear came running up to Thiessen and saluted. "They've broken through topside. Total control up there. No exits. And there's a lot of them. I'd say seventy-five or more. There's no way we can hold them for more than a few minutes, so we've got pickets heading back toward the subtunnels."

"That will have to do." Thiessen turned to Marcus. She grabbed him by the arm and pulled him aside. "There's a ventilation shaft on the bottom level. It runs the length of the old line, so you should be able to take it as far as you need to. If I'm not with you, you have to take care of Alexandra. That has to be your priority. There's an ammo dump we use in the basement of the old bus station on Eastern Ave., just outside the Silver Spring stop. Whoever makes it out knows to rendezvous there."

"And then what?"

Thiessen shook her head. "It's over for us. We did all we could, but I guess in the end we never had much of a chance, you know?" She grinned, a sad, hopeless smile. "You get 'em clear, and then you take care of her. That's what you do."

Another explosion echoed from somewhere above. More armed men ran past and took up positions along the concrete barrier beside the two scared boys.

"Promise me."

Marcus hesitated for only a moment. "I promise."

Thiessen looked him in the eyes and saw that he meant it. She slapped him once on the chest, and then walked over to Alexandra. She hugged the girl tight. If she was scared, Alexandra didn't show it, but there were tears in Thiessen's eyes. "I love you, Faðirin," she said, using the familiar nickname Marcus had only heard once before. "Take care of yourself, you understand? I'll see you again." She put her palm flat on the girl's chest and held it there, bowing her head and whispering a silent prayer. She looked up at Marcus and nodded.

He took Alexandra's hand, and all hell broke loose.

* * *

After they blew the wall, Dominic was the first one in. Past the smoke and the dust and the falling rocks was an antechamber that led to a black hole where the ancient escalators were. Dominic remembered it from the old days before the war, when he'd come as a child to the Wheaton station to ride that escalator, one of the longest and deepest in the world.

And he also remembered the stories of how people fled to Wheaton from the marauding Ashkhani on the day of The Rising. They were scared, panicked. They pushed and they shoved until someone slipped and the moving stairway became a waterfall of bodies, a cascade of death, ending in a pool of blood, flesh, and broken bones.

"They won't be in the station," Harrington said. "Can't defend it. They'll be set up in the maintenance tunnels off the main hallway."

"Agreed. Let's go. And watch your step."

Dominic was on point as the team descended the stairwell, the lights from their helmets bouncing up and down and threatening to disorient them. So when Dominic's light suddenly seemed to come to a dead stop in front of him, he thought he was losing his mind.

Harrington cursed. "It's a wall. They blocked it off halfway down."

Dominic couldn't help but grin. "Well I'll be damned."

"Shit, Dom, I told you we should have been quiet. We'll have to back off and blow this, too. They could have a whole army set up down there by the time we get through."

"Don't worry about it, darling. I don't think you can imagine how scared they are right now."

He turned back and shouted an order up the escalator. They retreated up the incline, waiting until the demolition crew gave the sign. The explosion was much louder than before, and Dominic wondered if the whole tunnel might come down on top of them. When it didn't, he shouted an order and they started back down again. He could smell the fear rising from below, and he shuddered to imagine what Harrington would think if she could see his face. He leapt down the stairs, finally landing with a thud on the old, polished stone floors of the abandoned station.

Then he held up a fist, and everyone came to a stop. He listened, and watched, and noticed a pale light emanating from beneath a door off to his right. He signaled for his men to follow him, and he made his way to the edge of the tunnel, this time doing his best to keep quiet. The door was cracked open, and Dominic could see that it led to a ramp heading to the tunnels below. He turned and gave the "go" signal. The enemy was out there, and they would meet them with overwhelming force.

He eased the door open and stepped through, but wasn't shot immediately, which was a good sign. The others filed in behind him. They gathered at the top of the ramp. Dominic could even make out voices now from below. He nodded to Harrington, then he removed a grenade from his belt and she did the same. They pulled the pins and lobbed them down into the darkness.

* * *

Marcus heard the grenade bouncing down the slope before he saw it. He grabbed Alexandra and threw her behind a concrete barricade. "Get down!" he yelled as he dove after her. The explosion was followed by another and then a roar that rode on a wave of gunfire. He swung his gun over the top of the barricade and aimed at muzzle flashes. Bullets slammed into concrete, men and women cried out in pain, and Marcus tried to ignore the fact that the next second could be his last. It was the war all over again.

Alexandra was beside him before he knew it. She used the rifle expertly, choosing her shots carefully. Bullets whizzed by her head, but she barely flinched. Marcus took the length of a breath, even in that chaos, to wonder what kind of life could forge a girl like that.

Another explosion went off, and in the brief light he saw Dominic. He'd taken a position toward the top of the ramp, standing there, for God and all his creatures to see, his gun spitting death and destruction. Harrington was there, too, farther down behind a fallen concrete beam, directing her troops. Two of Marcus's men were already down, but he and Alexandra had done a good job of making the Shepherds fall back. They had been too aggressive, and they'd paid for it in their dead. But Marcus knew they couldn't hold them for much longer.

"We have to go!" he screamed in Alexandra's ear.

"We can't," she said. She never took her eyes off the sight of her gun. "We move from here, we're dead."

She was right, but that didn't change things. "Well, we can't stay here."

"Agreed."

Alexandra looked across the open gulf between her and Thiessen. The two women's eyes met. Alexandra nodded, and Thiessen smiled.

"Take care of her!" Thiessen shouted above the roar.

"Wait, what's she doing?"

"What she must," Alexandra said. "Get ready to go."

Thiessen stood up and raked the ramp across from her with fire. She didn't stop until the rifle click-click-clicked empty. She threw the gun to the ground, and then she roared. Marcus watched in horror as she leapt over the barrier and ran toward Harrington. One bullet caught her, and then another, but she didn't stop running, not until Marcus was blinded by the flash and deafened by the roar that seemed to erupt from her body.

* * *

From his position at the top of the slope, Dominic saw the woman charging toward them. He knew what it meant. He zeroed in on her with his rifle, planning to cut her in half. But when he pulled the trigger, his gun jammed.

"No," he whispered. She caught a bullet and then another, but nothing that would stop her. Dominic took a step forward, but the flash that followed and the concussion that ripped through the concrete-ribbed chamber blew him back and threw him on the ground. But not before he saw Harrington rip apart, leaving only a fine, pink mist behind.

* * *

Marcus ducked behind the concrete barrier, but even then the blast managed for a moment to take away his sight and his hearing and his balance. He picked himself up and stumbled to his feet, and in the silence that followed, he surveyed a scene of carnage and fire unlike any he had witnessed since the war. He took the girl's hand. "Let's go."

They headed back into the tunnels, flanked by a cadre of armed men. But before they passed into the darkness and away from that place, a man roared.

"Marrrrcussss!"

He turned back to see Dominic, his body and clothes covered in dust, blood pouring from a gash in his skull, his face contorted in rage. The two men glared at each other. No words were needed. Marcus turned, and pulling Alexandra behind him, fled into the underground.

The Reborn

Chapter 25

They ran through a tunnel of darkness, deep beneath the city, their feeble lights able to do very little in that tomb, those one-day catacombs of an ancient city. The men set off charges as they went, bringing down the chambers behind them in the hopes of stymieing any pursuer. It was a wise precaution, even if Marcus thought it altogether unnecessary. Dominic wasn't coming after them, not today. He would wait, and bide his time.

They would meet again.

They reached the old bus depot after sun down. There were twenty of them, including Alexandra and Jacob the ex-data tech. The others were soldiers, covered in dust and blood and sweat. Marcus shook his head; it was a miracle they made it out. A miracle that Thiessen had engineered.

"They were with her," Alexandra said, "in the war."

She didn't say the colonel's name. She didn't have to.

"Did you know?" Marcus asked.

Alexandra pulled herself up onto a dirty ledge that had once served as a ticket counter. "Did I know that she was going to do that? I knew she was prepared to. I knew she was prepared to do just about anything to protect me. Do you disapprove?"

Marcus thought about it. "No," he said finally. "No, not at all."

"She always said that there was nothing more important than finding something you were willing to die for. She was a soldier, there's no doubt about that."

Chapter 26

Marcus led the way through the dank sewer tunnels that snaked their way to the ruins of the United Brick Corporation. The others followed behind, keeping close, waiting for an attack that could come at any moment.

They proceeded in absolute silence, the trickle of water reminding Marcus of a forest in winter. Devoid of life, but peaceful somehow.

Jacob navigated, following an old and faded sewer map that might have been up-to-date thirty years before. Marcus had his doubts, he couldn't deny that. But as much as things had changed on the surface, he had a feeling that the hidden underground of the city remained untouched.

Jacob held up a hand. "If we're where I think we are, we've got a turn and a couple hundred yards until we are underneath the heart of the facility. An old building like that would have a sewer access in its basement. They picked the old brick company for a reason. The warehouse had an underground storage facility. That's where they put the mainframes. When we pop up, we should be in the middle of the data room. Now, are you sure this isn't a trap?"

Marcus grinned at Jacob in the glow of his flashlight. "It's a trap all right. Dominic will be there. Waiting."

* * *

Dominic stood on a catwalk above the mainframes in the shadow of a concrete pillar, peaking around occasionally to see if the metal grate that covered the sewer access hatch was still in place. It was, for now. But he knew Marcus was coming. He could feel him.

The tactical team waited nervously behind him. All of them were hidden. Dominic wanted Marcus to feel comfortable, to bring his whole team in before he sprung the trap. Then it would be a massacre.

"Come back, Dominic."

Dominic clicked the switch on his earpiece and answered. "Yeah?"

"Up top is still clear. You sure they're coming?"

How Dominic already missed Harrington. She always had his back. Her replacement was . . . less reliable.

"I'm sure, Wiler. But he's not coming from up there."

Commander Porter had insisted that Marcus might try an attack from the surface, and he had made Dominic divide his forces equally to counter it. He was a fool, but Dominic didn't have time to care. Marcus was on a suicide mission, and Dominic was more than ready to oblige.

* * *

They reached the sewer cover without incident. Marcus was relieved; the tight spaces and narrow tunnels had seemed like a perfect place for an ambush. And yet nothing. Perhaps he had overestimated Dominic.

"I'll go first," he said to Jacob.

"You sure about that?"

"Somebody's gotta do it. If I get up there without getting shot, bring the rest of the team up."

"If we're lucky, maybe we can blow the place and get out before they even know we're here."

Marcus nodded. It was a nice thought, but he didn't think it was going to happen.

He reached up and pushed the manhole cover. At first it didn't budge, but then it gave way without a sound. A small victory. Marcus slid it over to the side, the ray of light that burst through from the surface growing bigger and brighter with every inch. He popped his head out of the opening and looked around. The great, electromagnetically-shielded computers hummed quietly around the room. Marcus marveled. Even if the war had set the world back in technology, this was an astounding amount of computing power. Everything one needed to catalogue every human being who had ever lived, call that information up in an instant, and deliver a death sentence.

Marcus signaled down to the men below. They climbed out of the hole one by one, with Jacob taking up the rear. Standing in the empty room, Marcus felt completely exposed.

"All right," he said to Jacob, "set up the explosives and let's get out of here. How long you need?"

"Five minutes, tops."

"Get to work."

But that work had not even started when the sound of clapping broke the silence and reverberated like thunder off the hard metal walls.

* * *

Dominic watched as they filed up from the sewer. Marcus stood in the center of the chamber like a fool, and Dominic could have killed him five times over before he even knew he was dead. It was almost too easy.

The girl wasn't with him. That, Dominic couldn't even believe. He'd assumed that after everything Marcus had done, all the bad decisions, he would simply deliver her up to Dominic for the slaughter. But it was no matter. With Marcus and her protectors dead, he would find her soon enough. Marcus had brought Dominic's prey within his sights. If he hadn't known better, he'd have thought Marcus was in on it, that this was all part of some greater plan.

Dominic signaled to his men to be ready. The last of the group had come up from the underground. There were fewer of them than he had expected, only a dozen maybe. Dominic considered calling Wiler from the surface, but thought better of it. He had more than enough men, and he didn't want to share the glory with anyone.

Dominic was done waiting. He rose from his position behind a stone column and stepped out onto the landing overlooking the mainframes. Then he started to clap.

*   *   *

And so it begins, Marcus thought. He looked up to see Dominic standing above him, mocking Marcus with his hands. His rifle was slung around his neck, his Spiker still hung from his belt.

"Well done, Marcus. Well done," he said, as others melted out of the shadows from above, their machine guns trained on Marcus and his men. "You brought them right to us. So much easier than hunting you down."

"Yeah, that didn't work out too well for you last time, did it?"

Dominic showed him his palms. "What can I say? We don't deal in madness. That's your side, remember? The kamikaze attack was unexpected, but you'll be happy to know, I'm sure, that you managed to kill some good people with it."

"Just trying to survive, Dominic. You know that. We wanted no part of it. You were the one who came to us."

Dominic leaned forward on the railing, his arms spread wide. "Marcus, what the hell are you doing? What the hell went wrong with you?"

"My eyes are open. I know the truth now."

"Truth? I'll tell you the truth. We're barely keeping it together. This country is hanging by a thread, and if that thread breaks we take the whole world down with us into a new dark age. That's a fact. That's the truth. But we also got a shot at something even better than just getting by. It's not like it was before the war, Marcus. Punk kids killing old folks on their own front porch for a couple bucks cash. The streets not safe to walk down at night. Children abducted, raped, murdered. All that's in the past now. We've made it a bad dream, more nightmare than reality. Isn't that worth something?"

"But it's all a lie, Dominic, and you know it. The Reborn? The Marked? You don't even know who they are . . . or who they really were."

Dominic grinned, and then he began to laugh. "You are so naïve. So simple-minded. It's so much bigger than that. You would have learned that, one day, if you had held on. If you hadn't failed. You would have learned the truth. The cancer that's all around us, eating us up. The same cancer that brought the world to its knees. It'll come back too, Marcus. *They* will come back, if we don't cut out the disease, if we don't stop them first. And that's our real job. That's what we really do.

"Do you know why they call us Shepherds, Marcus? Because someone has to cull the herd."

There was a rumble from above.

"So I'm sorry, but I think the time for conversation is at an end. I'm going to deal with you, and then I'm going to find that little bitch and cut her throat."

"Oh don't worry," Marcus said. "I think she's going to find you first. In fact, she should be around any moment."

Dominic paused, holding his rifle halfway up to his shoulder, a look of confusion spreading over his face. Then that confusion turned to clarity. Marcus smiled anyway. It was already too late.

The entire building shuddered, and an explosion ripped through the chamber.

* * *

The guard on duty outside the old brick corporation didn't know what it was when he first heard it, so out of place was the roar of a diesel engine. And then when he saw it tearing around the bend— an eighteen-wheeler hauling a massive tanker behind it going as fast as its engine would carry it—he began to believe that his eyes deceived him. He watched as it smashed into the metal gate, tearing the previously sturdy bars apart like they were made of aluminum foil. He didn't even think to call it in, stumbling dumbly after the truck instead as the tanker rumbled toward the warehouse that served as headquarters. It was only when the tanker didn't slow down, when it smashed through the metal walls and kept going, when the sound of autoguns opening up on the behemoth intruder erupted, that he turned around and started to run back toward his post to call for backup.

He ran headlong into the girl. He stumbled backwards and nearly fell. She looked at him and smiled. Then she raised her gun and shot him twice in the chest. The last thing he saw was a bloom of orange fire. The last thing he heard was the sound of the autoguns swallowed up in an explosion that carried him away into darkness.

* * *

Orange light flashed across Dominic's enraged face before a sonic boom threw him to the ground. The explosion was bigger than Marcus had expected. So big that it blew him across the room, sliding him along the floor and slamming his back into a wall. A bloom of fire roared from above, and Marcus was afraid he'd underestimated and that they were all about to be roasted alive. But then the vortex reversed, with air and flame filling the vacuum that the detonation of C-4 and 10,000 gallons of gasoline had carved. The roar of the inferno was replaced with another sound—Dominic's fury.

He pulled himself to his feet, his face covered with black soot, his hair singed, and jerked his rifle up to his shoulder. He began to fire; battle was engaged.

His men joined him one at a time, as each managed to recover from the shock. Shots exploded and bullets ricocheted off of walls and floors and the metal shielding that covered the computer mainframes. Marcus was glad for them, as they provided the only cover for the men below. They needed it, too. With Dominic roaring above, they were like fish in a barrel. Alexandra was on her way with reinforcements, but with the fire still raging on the surface, who knew how long she might be.

He swung his rifle back and forth along the top of the metal case he was hiding behind, firing blindly. "It's over Dominic! It's over!" Machine-gun fire answered him. There was a pause, and

Marcus peeked around the corner of the mainframe, only to see Dominic standing directly in front of him.

He'd leapt from the overhead railing, landing with a thud and rolling forward, regaining his footing just as Marcus appeared. Dominic reached back and punched him right in the face.

Marcus felt his nose break, blood and mucus clouding his vision even as he fell backwards in shock and pain. "You son of a bitch." Dominic kicked him in the stomach. "You turned your back on everything."

He swung again with his foot, but this time, Marcus was ready. He grabbed the other man's leg, pulling back and falling forward at the same time. Dominic lost his balance and pitched over.

Marcus wasn't sure exactly what all happened then. It was a fury of punching and biting, wild swings and kicks. But Dominic was getting the better of it. Marcus felt something break inside of him. The Spiker swung past his hand from Dominic's hip and he reached for it. But Dominic was too fast.

"No, no, no, not this time." He pushed Marcus back to the ground and flung the Spiker far away from them. Marcus used every last bit of strength to lunge at Dominic. A gun fired. Marcus felt a dull stinging in his gut just as he wrapped his arms around Dominic. His strength left him, and he found himself sliding to the floor. A circle of red blood spread from the open wound in Marcus's stomach.

Dominic stood over him, grinning. He shook his head.

"Call it what you will, Marcus. God. Fate. Genetics. But in the end, we all get what we deserve."

He raised the gun and aimed it at Marcus's head. Marcus glared back at him and waited for death.

But then something happened.

Dominic's body jerked. Confusion replaced fury. Two metal prongs burst from his chest, spraying blood on Marcus. The light faded from Dominic's eyes before he collapsed to his knees and then fell down to his side, the Spiker jammed in his back.

Alexandra stood looking down at him.

It was only then that Marcus realized the sounds of battle had ceased. The Shepherds who had survived the explosion above had been neutralized. Jacob was attaching explosives to the mainframes.

It was over.

"Faðirin!" someone called, "we did it!"

And then Marcus remembered something that he had not meant to forget.

He looked up at Alexandra.

"That name," he said, "what does it mean?"

For a moment she paused, looking at him but past him at the same time. The blood flowed out of his body, and the air hung heavy.

"It's an old word," she said, "from ancient times." She reached down and picked up the gun that Dominic had been carrying. "It is a very special name. A great name." She popped out the clip and, seeing that it was not empty, jammed it back into the gun. "It is, I suppose, the first word ever spoken." She smiled. "It means . . ." She pulled back the slide, chambering a round.

"Father."

The End

Brett J. Talley is the Bram Stoker Award nominated author of *That Which Should Not Be* and *The Void*. His work has been featured in the shared-world anthology, *Limbus, Inc.*, and he is the editor of the forthcoming sequel, *Limbus 2*. He is also a lawyer, speechwriter, and an avid fan of the Alabama Crimson Tide. He makes his internet home on his website, www.brettjtalley.com.